SPECIAL MESSAGE TO READERS

THE ULVERSCROFT FOUNDATION
(registered UK charity number 264873)
was established in 1972 to provide funds for research, diagnosis and treatment of eye diseases. Examples of major projects funded by the Ulverscroft Foundation are:-

- The Children's Eye Unit at Moorfields Eye Hospital, London
- The Ulverscroft Children's Eye Unit at Great Ormond Street Hospital for Sick Children
- Funding research into eye diseases and treatment at the Department of Ophthalmology, University of Leicester
- The Ulverscroft Vision Research Group, Institute of Child Health
- Twin operating theatres at the Western Ophthalmic Hospital, London
- The Chair of Ophthalmology at the Royal Australian College of Ophthalmologists

You can help further the work of the Foundation by making a donation or leaving a legacy. Every contribution is gratefully received. If you would like to help support the Foundation or require further information, please contact:

THE ULVERSCROFT FOUNDATION
The Green, Bradgate Road, Anstey
Leicester LE7 7FU, England
Tel: (0116) 236 4325

website: www.foundation.ulverscroft.com

THE LAVENDER FIELD

Having rejected a marriage proposal, Mel Sanderson takes a job at the Villa Lavanda on Croatia's beautiful coast. Makso, the owner, is overbearing, whilst his Japanese wife Hiroko keeps herself to herself. When Mel finds a note thrown onto her balcony — a message bearing the desperate words *PLEASE. HELP. ME.* — she can't just ignore it. But she is also in danger, with no idea of where to turn for help . . .

Books by Cara Cooper
in the Linford Romance Library:

SAFE HARBOUR
TAKE A CHANCE ON LOVE
THE SANCTUARY
HEALING LOVE
LEAVING HOME
TANGO AT MIDNIGHT
LOVE CASTAWAY
THE LEMON GROVE

CARA COOPER

THE LAVENDER FIELD

Complete and Unabridged

LINFORD
Leicester

First published in Great Britain in 2016

First Linford Edition
published 2017

A catalogue record for this book is available from the British Library.

ISBN 978–1–4448–3291–4

Published by
F. A. Thorpe (Publishing)
Anstey, Leicestershire

Set by Words & Graphics Ltd.
Anstey, Leicestershire
Printed and bound in Great Britain by
T. J. International Ltd., Padstow, Cornwall

This book is printed on acid-free paper

1

Mel felt decidedly under-dressed. A grey suit and crisp white shirt had looked great when she'd boarded the plane from London. 'Businesslike and neat' was the image she'd wanted. Now, here at a country Villa in Croatia, it felt dull and downbeat. Why had she ever imagined it would look right for an interview with a man like Maksimiljan Yurcich?

True, she had known her prospective new employer was rich, a mega-successful producer of wine, olive oil and lavender. But she hadn't realised that the Villa Lavanda was quite so splendid.

Mel's taxi negotiated the winding driveway up the hill. She unfolded the job advert she'd seen six weeks ago, creases worn into it. It had been a dream then. A new life, a route to happiness after the trauma of turning down Cesare's marriage proposal. On a wet day in London, the notice had jumped out at her from the newspaper:

WANTED: RELIABLE INDIVIDUAL to be Personal Assistant to businessman residing in Croatia

You will act as general factotum/aide de camp in helping this successful entrepreneur manage his interests. These include fields for the production of lavender oil products, olive oil plantations, and wine production. This is an interesting and varied post. In addition, the successful candidate will act as companion to this gentleman's young wife who has had her first baby. There is a nurse/nanny to look after the child: you will be the back-up when the nurse is absent on leave. You will be organised, have a pleasant outgoing personality, and relish hard work. This is not a post for someone who wants set hours — flexibility is a must. In return,

Mr Macksimiljan Yurcich offers excellent conditions. These include a self-contained studio flat in the Villa Lavanda near the medieval town of Vodnjan. Also, the use of formal gardens, a swimming pool, and a path to a private beach where you can enjoy days off. A competitive salary is offered. If you meet these requirements, send a CV to The Villa Lavanda, Vodnjan, Istria, Croatia 94573. There will be interviews over Skype, and the shortlisted candidate will be offered a second interview in person with Mr Yurcich at The Villa. All expenses paid.

Mel folded the advert and placed it in her purse. As the taxi crunched along the drive, her eyes grew as wide as two-pound coins. It wasn't just the gold-tipped gates glistening in the sun at the estate's entrance. Nor was it the acres of olive trees planted in rows, or grape vines carefully tended by workers. As they approached the Villa, she rolled down the window and breathed in the heady scent of thousands of glorious lavender bushes, mauve stripes over sun-burned hills.

She smoothed her skirt. Modestly-priced, it now felt cheap. She wished she was more elegant. Particularly once the magnificent house came into view. Tucked behind fir trees, this was special. Master of its surroundings, painted peachy-cream, the Villa nestled coolly under its Cedar of Lebanon umbrella. A wooden overhang, supported by white pillars, created a veranda with cane seating. Bedrooms above had balconies with views to the sea, and in the distance was the harbour of Fazana and the port of Pula. Even the double-fronted door was splendid, a concoction in carved cherry-wood depicting lavender fronds and the family coat of arms.

Was it really only yesterday Mel had chatted about her future with her close friend Caroline? She'd been relaxed about the move from England to Croatia.

'So, you're ready, flight booked, case packed. Aren't you risking it by flying into Pula just six hours before your final interview?'

'The weather's perfect in July; there won't be delays. After a leisurely lunch, I'll catch a taxi to the Villa. Everything's sorted, it's cool.'

'So are you, Mel, like a cucumber. That's one of the reasons I'll miss you.' There was a catch in Caroline's throat. Mel wanted to change the subject though she felt the parting from her best friend just as badly. She wished they were saying goodbye in person rather than over the phone, Mel in London, Caroline in Italy. 'It's a short plane ride from Italy, Caro. You'll come out and see me. Remember we've got your wedding dress to choose.'

'But you've been looking after that brother of mine for fourteen years — and Izzy ... she's distraught at you going. You were like a mother to her. It's true she's nearly grown up, but we've known you a long time. I couldn't want a more precious friend. The time we spent in Sorrento together with you looking after Izzy while we sorted out that derelict beach house was such fun. Do you remember the time poor Antonio got stung by the jellyfish and we nursed him back to health? And those wonderful meals down at Beatrice's house in the lemon grove? Now he and I are glued to the Hotel Girasole, building up our business. I miss those days we all spent in Italy together.' Caroline had sniffed, holding back tears. 'Do you miss Cesare?'

Mel's breath caught as she remembered the wonderful Italian policeman who had wanted to marry her but who she'd had to turn down. 'Yes, but the time wasn't right, Caro. We all have to move on.'

Caroline hastily changed the subject. 'Let's hope this new job is right for you. Personal Assistant is a big step from being a nanny, and the role of companion to a rich man's wife is a tall order. Still, I know you'll love being around a baby again. When is Mrs Yurcich out of hospital?'

Maksimiljan Yurcich's young Japanese wife was called Hiroko. Mel suspected her to be delicate. He had asked Mel to call him Makso during the interview over Skype. He had revealed that his wife, Hiroko, had experienced a difficult pregnancy and a traumatic birth. But mother and baby boy were both doing well. During the interview, Mel had found Makso to be firm, a man in a hurry. He was fiercely protective of his son and wife. From the little Mel had seen of him on the tiny screen of her smartphone, he was skinny and rangy, with bony fingers which he ran through thick hair standing up from high temples. A strong broad nose and brooding brows made her think she would not like to be on the wrong side of Makso Yurcich.

She thought again of her chat with Caroline. 'Mrs Yurcich is out of hospital, but having to take bed rest. I know it's tough, my going away, but I need to make a new start.' Mel smiled to think of her former lover Cesare. She hadn't been able to accept the charming Italian's proposal of marriage; she wasn't ready to settle down. But maybe this trip and a new job would help her forget.

Mel bit her finger as the taxi stopped at the front door. This trip was important to her. She'd had to turn Cesare down. It wasn't that he wasn't kind, generous or startlingly good-looking. He was all that and more. It was his wish to settle and have babies right away.

For Mel, who'd been pronounced infertile following childhood leukaemia, meeting a man like Cesare, who burned to have children, was something she had dreaded. Fate could be cruel. To know you would fail a man like that was awful to contemplate. She hadn't told Cesare what had put her off marriage: it was too painful to discuss. Especially when all Mel wanted, coming from a large family, was children of her own. At sixteen years old, the consultant had told her that the cancer treatment had rendered her infertile. The bombshell rocked her to the core. Looking after other people's children was the closest Mel would get to having ones of her own. Unless, of course … Her hands formed into tight fists.

No. An expert had told her there was no hope. She was too practical to indulge in pipe dreams. Looking for miracles where there were none was a fool's errand.

Mel pictured Caroline and her handsome fiancé Antonio. They were due to be married shortly in the enchanting seaside resort of Sorrento — Antonio's childhood home. Caroline had confessed to Mel that one of the first things she wanted was a baby, and there was every chance she could be pregnant by Christmas. For Mel, who would only ever bounce other women's children on her knee, that made her feel as empty and barren as a desert. She'd give up all the riches on earth to have a child with Cesare.

She shook herself from her reverie. It wasn't to be. He must forget her, and find a good Italian woman with childbearing hips who could produce lots of bambinos. She must knuckle down to the job at hand, and enjoy life. This adventure would make her forget . . .

Cesare walked up the Girasole's steps carrying the panettone with dark chocolate filling he had baked that morning. He was drawn to Antonio's hotel like a moth to a flame. It was all he had left of Mel. The girl with the glossy chestnut hair and lips like English roses was even more on his mind since she had left. *Why, why, why?* He had asked that question a thousand times. Had he been too direct for her? Maybe he just didn't understand English girls.

'Cesare.' Antonio grasped him in a bear hug.

'Careful, this panettone took me hours to bake. It is a little gift, I was just passing.'

'Come, have coffee.' Antonio led him to where Caroline sat by the pool. Ever busy, she was sorting invoices in date order.

'Cesare!' She pecked him on the cheek. 'Can I pour you an espresso?'

As she cut the warm cake, chocolate goop oozed. 'I was wondering,' Cesare asked, licking his fingers, 'have you heard from Mel?'

'Not since you asked yesterday.' Caroline smiled.

'*Mi dispiace.* I worry for her. Do you think she is ok?'

Caroline fleetingly placed her hand on the back of his. 'I think she'll be fine. But she misses you.'

'She does?' A bud of hope opened at her words.

'She told me so.' Caroline refilled his cup.

'Maybe I should write. I . . . I thought she did not wish me to be in contact.'

'Not at all, Cesare. Whatever made you think that? I can't tell you why she went, but I do know she'd love to hear from you. Antonio and I shall be visiting her soon. Maybe, if you and she have corresponded, you might want to consider popping over with us?'

He was being thrown a lifeline. Antonio looked at him, nodding approval. All was not lost. 'Only if she wants,' Cesare said, but his heart was lighter. He picked up a second slice of panettone and ate it with gusto. Today was turning out to be a good one.

'Miss Melanie Sanderson?' A woman with black plain hair and a blue dress had been waiting on the steps of the Villa to greet her. She came over and spoke through the open car window. Beside her stood a young, studious-looking boy of around sixteen with dark eyes, an intelligent brow and a ready smile. But perhaps his most notable feature was a port-wine stain on his left cheek, the size of a tangerine, shaped like a map of France. As soon as he saw Mel, his hand went to his cheek automatically. Mel wished he wouldn't be self-conscious; he was such a good-looking boy. He ran to get her suitcase.

'Please call me Mel, everyone does.' As Mel climbed out of the air-conditioned car, the heat hit her like an oven door had opened.

Extending her arm, the woman's handshake was warm and genuine. 'I am Severina Vanka, my husband Ivan is the chauffeur, and this is my son Mihovil.

He will settle you in before your final interview with Mr Yurcich. I am sorry I have to rush off; I have things cooking which I must attend to.'

She looked harassed. Makso must be a hard taskmaster. Mel was feeling more uneasy as the interview loomed.

Mihovil gave a little bow. 'In English, my name would be Michael, but you can call me Mihovil if you choose.'

'I like Mihovil,' said Mel, 'it's a good strong name.'

Mihovil glowed. Mel guessed he was pleased his mother trusted him with this task. 'I wish to improve my English and learn about your country. You have come from London?'

'That's right.' Mel took care with her pronunciation: the boy looked keen to learn.

'I have been teaching myself off the television news. People speak very fast; I like that you speak slow.'

'You're doing very well. Your English is good. Have there been many other candidates?'

'About twelve women and a man. None have returned. You're last.'

Involuntarily, Mel gulped, her nervousness getting the better of her. They went into a small sitting room.

'Mr Yurcich is on a conference call. Can I make you tea? That is what you English like in the afternoon, isn't it?'

'Tea would be lovely, and I presume I'll be interviewed by Mrs Yurcich too if I am to be her companion?'

Mel saw Mihovil hesitate as if he didn't know what to say. Maybe his mother had warned him not to say too much. 'I don't know. Mrs Yurcich is not very well. Makso says she must not see anyone. She has been only with the nurse.'

'That's strange. I understood I was to be her companion. I want to help.'

'It is best if you ask Mr Yurcich about his wife.' Mihovil smiled.

Mel guessed there was far more going on in this household than was immediately obvious. Families so often involved secrets — she had learnt that through years of being a nanny. It wasn't fair to push him, and she certainly didn't want to get him into trouble. 'Is it just you and your mother who work here?'

'And my father.' Mihovil smiled, but she thought she saw a flicker of concern cross his face. 'If you don't mind, I must water the plants. I hope you have everything you need.'

What a serious young lad. Mel wondered about him long after he'd left. After waiting an interminable time, she got fidgety. Makso might be busy, but she wasn't going to wait forever. The afternoon was waning. If she was going to be sent home (she was sure she wouldn't be chosen for the job) she'd need to catch a plane soon. She'd get a cancellation if she wasn't at the airport too late.

Mel, never one to be inactive, believed in making things happen. Creeping into the long passage, no one was around. If she walked further towards the back of the house, she might find someone.

The interior of the Villa was even more impressive here. Alcoves in the wall, with spotlights within, displayed superb Croatian artefacts. A terracotta bull in colours of parched earth — ochre, sandstone and burnt umber. Opposite, Mel was captivated by a carved head of a beautiful girl. A simple masterpiece so well-executed you could have reached out to touch the curled hair, the delicate chiselled eyebrows. Without thinking, she did just that.

From behind her, a loud voice boomed: 'I wouldn't do that — all my treasures are alarmed.'

She held her hand to her chest and saw the solid frame of Makso Yurcich darken the passage.

His face was long, with brows hooding his eyes like cliff edges. With not an ounce of spare flesh, his jaw and cheekbones were pronounced, and two deep lines ran from the corners of his nose to the edges of his mouth.

'But I can understand your wish to feel the artistry of the sculpture. She is very fine, isn't she? Modelled with love by a sculptor who must have known she would outlive him by thousands of years.

She's from the third century AD, carved in pink alabaster.'

'I didn't mean to be nosey. I got worried I'd been forgotten. Forgive me.'

'I cannot condemn someone for having a healthy interest in art. It is my passion. My apologies, I had an urgent call. Now you see why I need an assistant — there aren't enough hours in the day. Pleased to make your acquaintance finally.' He held out his hand, and for some reason, she hesitated to be taken in his hold. His presence was so domineering. He was the sort of man who would hush a room by walking into it. She felt her hand encompassed in icy fingers. His grip was tight. He released her. 'Come to my office. We will talk business.'

Makso's office was neat and controlled, like its owner. He sat down in a black leather swivel chair beside a window which looked out on to a sparkling swimming pool. He bid Mel to sit at the smaller chair opposite, in front of a leather-topped desk. Along the wall, glass-fronted display cases held books ranging from art reference works to some on property, trade and farming. They summed up everything: how Makso made his money, and how he spent it.

'So . . .' He steepled his hands. Mel perched on the edge of her seat. Surely now he saw her cut-price suit, her chestnut hair falling unstyled about her shoulders, and would know she was unsuitable. 'We have met, as it were, on Skype. What do you think of my estate?' He waved his hand theatrically.

'It's beautiful. Very impressive.'

'I'm glad you think so. I've worked hard to achieve my aims. I do not tolerate shirkers or malingerers. Are you a malingerer?'

'Certainly not. I work hard for my employers. I spent the last fourteen years as nanny to a delightful girl, Izzy, who's grown up into a bright, happy individual. I didn't just look after her, I kept house for her father, Oscar Beaumont, a prominent lawyer. Izzy's mother died when she was young. I also cooked, shopped, and cleaned Oscar's London flat. I think I can say that they've come to be friends.'

'That is a firm testimonial. You have spirit. I like that. I am also impressed that you regard friendship as important. My wife ...' He looked across the swathes of lavender to the distant sea. '... is unwell.'

'Unwell?'

'The birth was difficult. It was not all it was meant to be, in her mind. There was a degree of medical intervention which has left her ... ' He stopped. His mouth moved, but nothing came out. For the first time, Mel felt sorry for this powerful man. However much money he had, he still had problems. Everything looked perfect in this glossy house, but it was a facade.

'The trauma of birth has left her dejected. She has no spirit for life and I fear she may neglect our son.'

'I'm sure that wouldn't happen, Mr Yurcich.'

'Makso, I am Makso to everyone. My friends. Even my enemies.'

'I'm sure that wouldn't happen.' Mel

repeated herself; he might be master here, but she had more experience of mothers and children. She had trained at the famous Norland College for nannies, and its motto, 'Love Never Faileth', had been her guide. 'Could it be that what you are describing is post-natal depression?'

He paced the room. His feet in their Italian leather shoes trod silently on the thick white carpet. 'Top doctors have made their pronouncements, done their tests. What they have not done is made my wife better. You see, Hiroko, my little Japanese flower, was full of sadness even before the birth of our son, Ivo. There was a sickness in her mind before she became pregnant. I believed that having a child, which was her greatest wish, would cure her. She told me that was what she wanted, and I believed her. Now, she leaves Ivo in his cot and lets the nurse tend him. Such neglect isn't natural.'

Mel listened intently. As she did, her own heart felt tight in her chest. Feelings of sadness and regret at her childlessness were raw. She felt for the young woman she had never met.

At that point, like a Greek chorus in a tragedy, the sound of a crying baby filtered into the room. Makso halted, then continued to pace. His eyes narrowed. 'My son needs a proper mother. A wife has obligations.' He winced at the crying, the lines on his face deepening, the shadows about his jaw blackening. This man required obedience. The inability of his wife to care for their son went against the grain. Mel was desperate to be of use. Now, far from thinking this job might slip through her fingers, she was determined to win it. She hadn't come all this way to be defeated.

The crying became more insistent. 'Where is that nurse?' His voice raised a notch.

'Mr Yurcich … ' He glared at Mel. 'Sorry. Makso. I believe I can help your wife. I can be her companion and guide her. I have experience, both actual and theoretical. I've read everything there is to read about childcare, I've practised it, and have even written articles and been asked to lead seminars on the subject back in England. But I never wanted to teach. I wanted to *do.* I also have compassion. If you let me help you and your wife, you won't regret it. I'm also very happy to handle your business affairs as your personal assistant. Once your wife and I get to know each other, I can bring her out of her shell, and then hopefully she won't need me any more. I can balance the two roles. I'll work hard — I realise this isn't a nine-to-five job. Please, would there be any chance I could meet your wife?'

Grey eyes bored into her like they could see into her soul. The baby had been calmed. There was no more crying. 'That was an impassioned speech. Of all the candidates I have seen for this role, none have spoken like you. I was beginning to lose hope that the right person would come along. In fact, I think I have found her. Miss Sanderson, you're hired as from this moment.'

He marched over to a bell in the wall, and in a minute, Severina and Mihovil appeared. 'Please take Miss Sanderson to her accommodation. She will be staying.'

Mel felt her bottom lip tremble, but fought to control herself. This was to be her new home, this luxurious house in this wonderful country, and there was work to be done. She wanted to reach out, grab his hand and hold it. Instead, she stood straight. 'Thank you. You won't regret it.'

'I hope not.' His expression was grave, as if troubles weighed heavy on his shoulders. The phone rang and he turned, closing the door, and leaving Mel to follow Severina and Mihovil. It was only at that point, as they walked up a wide staircase and along the corridor, that Mel realised he had completely ignored her request to meet his wife.

The next few days were a whirlwind of activity. Mel flew back to London, and whizzed off letters here, there and everywhere to let people know that she was, for the foreseeable future, to be living in sunny Croatia. Oscar was sweet as always, treating her to a luxurious farewell dinner, with Izzy wearing a new dress and looking so, so grown-up. There were tears, but mainly of joy for her new beginning. And before she knew it, Mel was back, and the Villa Lavanda had become her new home.

Greg Bodie had been fixing some loose tiles near the swimming pool. As he trowelled on cement, he strained to hear what was being said through the window in Makso's study. He'd watched a succession of hopefuls troop in, only to be shown straight out. The small, brisk woman in there now though had stayed for longer than any of them. He couldn't make out what she was saying, but she was feisty — and, Greg decided, might actually be a match for Makso. As Greg gathered together his tools and stood up, he was just in time to see them shake hands, and Mihovil be called in to take her luggage upstairs.

So, he pondered as he made his way back to the tool shed. There was to be another member of the household. Would that make his job easier, or more difficult — might she get in the way? He locked the shed door and walked off to wash his hands. That would remain to be seen, wouldn't it? He'd just have to keep his eye on her, wouldn't he?

Mel woke with a start. She had left her curtains open and a glorious dawn was painting the horizon in raspberry-ripple pinks. For a moment she had the feeling you get on holiday of not knowing which bed you're in. Even though she had now been at the Villa one full night, it still felt like a dream.

She threw open the doors. Here on the first floor, with her own balcony, it felt too good to be true. The breaking sun winked on the sea in the distance. The gentle sound of the swimming-pool pump clicking into life was a million miles from London's traffic. A perfect day beckoned.

Insomnia was something she had always lived with, but it didn't worry her. In fact, she embraced it. For a woman who lived a busy life with children, these golden peaceful early hours were a bonus.

The rest of the household was unlikely to be up for ages. What she really fancied was a walk before the world got going. She closed the French windows, got dressed, and made her way downstairs. Severina had explained to her how to set and unset the burglar alarm. Mihovil had shown Mel the keys to the bike shed, so Mel pulled one out and started cycling.

'In this direction,' Mihovil had pointed south, 'is the path through the olive and lavender fields to Makso's private beach. The town of Fazana is by road over in that direction. It's only half an hour to cycle there — it's a gentle slope downhill. But, coming back, it's uphill all the way, and not to be done in the heat of the day.'

'What's Fazana like?'

'I love it — there's seaside with a white pebble beach which looks out on the Brijuni islands. The Brijuni were President Tito's playground, with a safari park with zebras and an elephant, no cars allowed. You must visit; my grandfather keeps a boat in Fazana.

'In the other direction, if you take the unmarked paths through the fields, you can reach Makso's private beach. There's a landing stage — Makso's yacht is moored there. The private cove is closer than Fazana, maybe ten minutes to cycle from here. Some of the paths are overgrown, and you are an English city lady, so you will not understand the countryside. You must be careful.'

Mel remembered his quaint concern, as she cycled round the edges of the fields. Sun settled on the lavender which exuded its pungent scent. Mel filled her lungs, overjoyed to be alive. The further she got from the house, the more scrubby the land became, with prickly weeds and endless winding paths. She followed one, heading for the sea. She'd set herself a challenge to pedal to Makso's private beach. Once she'd settled in, if she had leisure time she would love to bring a picnic and bathe in the sea as she had done in Sorrento with Caroline, Antonio and Izzy. She only hoped there were no jellyfish off the Croatian coast!

The paths got narrower, and Mel felt her legs brushed by dry grasses which clattered in the spokes. The way had got uneven, but luckily the bike was up to it. She just wasn't sure her bottom was! As she rounded a bend, she stopped, startled. Over to her right, above the sea, appeared a collection of small round houses. Around twenty of them nestled in a dip, as if someone had built them to stay hidden. She remembered them from her guidebook. Trullo houses could be ancient, and were built of bleached stone, with slate-coloured roofs. She wondered if they were medieval ruins, then realised they were inhabited. Washing hung out in the still air. Curious, she thought, that anyone should live out here miles away from civilisation. There wasn't a shop, a telephone box, or even a road in sight. The only way to the trulli was along these unmade paths. What did these people do for a living? How did they get to hospital if they were ill?

Pondering, she resumed pedalling. It wasn't much longer to the sea. As she rode, she looked back. The trulli were totally hidden. The way became more difficult — sharp things grabbed at her bare legs — but she was determined to complete her mission. The sun climbed in a cloudless sky and she began to sweat. She hadn't had anything to eat, and was becoming lightheaded with the exercise.

Mel pedalled madly, becoming increasingly disoriented. She only saw the long black snake crossing her path out of the corner of her eye. But, it was enough to make her shriek and overreact. Her yell rang through the silent air. She slammed on her brakes, and crashed headlong into a pile of thorn bushes. As she lay, the snake's head turned. Mel stared helplessly at it. It opened its jaws. She went to scream again when she heard a man's voice, in a calm and measured whisper: 'Don't panic and don't move a muscle.'

Mel stayed silent, not even sure she could speak. She didn't dare breathe. The voice behind her said, 'There are only two poisonous snakes in Croatia, the adder and the nose-horned viper. Don't make any sudden movements and you'll stay safe. Can you get up without any jerky movements?'

Mel eyed the snake. The snake eyed her. 'Yes, probably.' Then she gasped. 'My leg's bleeding, I've been bitten.'

Gradually the young man moved into view. He had curly sandy hair, and frowned intently at her bleeding leg through heavy-rimmed Michael Caine spectacles. Over his left shoulder was flung a leather man-bag. He wore workman's clothes, jeans and a denim shirt. He brandished a stick between her and the snake. 'Stand up very slowly … here, use my arm to steady you.'

'Is that snake one of the poisonous ones?'

'Difficult to tell.' He didn't bat an eyelid. 'I don't know what they look like. One thing I do know is that the nose-horned viper isn't keen on water.' With that, as if in slow motion, he took out a bottle and handed it to her. 'Here, give him a good sprinkling.'

With shaking hands, she did as she was told. One douche of water and the snake slithered into the undergrowth with a rattle of dry grass. She clung to the young man's hand for support, her legs like spaghetti. 'Was that a poisonous one?'

He washed her calf with the bottled water. 'Well, he did have the tell-tale zigzag markings and that cute little nose like a hook.'

'You said you weren't an expert!'

'Sometimes I lie to protect the innocent.'

She laughed, despite her anxiety. 'Have I been bitten?'

'No. You'll live, you've just got a nasty thorn in your leg.' He whipped out the offending thorn, took a clean handkerchief, and tied it tightly where he'd cleaned her skin.

'Thank heavens. And thank *you*. What would I have done if you weren't here?'

'Picked up your bike and gone on your

way. Most snakes, even the ones that bite, have no interest in attacking; they mind their own business unless provoked. Their main interests are mice, lizards, or a juicy bird. I've seen them a few times hereabouts. He was probably more terrified of you than you were of him.'

'I don't know about that.' She held her hand to her throat.

'You're going to have some nasty bruises. Are you ok?'

'I'm fine, thanks. It's my pride that's wounded. I owe you one, as long as you don't tell anyone what a twerp I've been.'

'Not at all. Can I walk you somewhere ... where have you come from?'

'The Villa Lavanda.'

'Ah, so you're the prim English miss! I'm going back there myself. Greg Bodie, handyman/gardener to the great Makso Yurcich, at your service. Give me your bike. That wheel's buckled; you won't be going anywhere on it today.'

Greg hauled the bike upright. It wouldn't take him long to fix. The girl limped beside him. She was shaken, but not one to dwell on misfortune. He admired her for regaining her cool. 'You're the new secretary and companion to Mrs Yurcich. Mel Sanderson isn't it?'

'That's right.' She had an engaging smile, and glowing peaches-and-cream skin untouched by the sun. He guessed some Irish parentage had given her those luminous eyes. She seemed to be weighing him up as she spoke. 'News travels fast in Croatia.'

'We like a good gossip below stairs. Severina told me of your arrival; she's pleased to have another woman around. The Villa Lavanda can be a bit macho with Makso at its helm.' She smiled but said nothing. Fiercely loyal, he noted. That could be a good thing, or a bad thing, depending ... 'And have you met the missus yet?'

'Not yet. I want to.'

'How's that leg?'

'Fine, thank you. How long have you been here?'

'Just six months. I'm all settled in now.

I help out Ivan — Severina's husband — with the car, and fix stuff around the house. I'm teaching Mihovil things, he's a bright kid. I do the pool and a bit of gardening. It beats mouldering away in Southampton.'

'What did you do there?'

'Worked in the shipyard — welding, engineering. I got out before they closed it, I saw the writing on the wall. My mates weren't so lucky. They have families to feed, it's been tough on them. I feel a total charlatan out here in the sun.'

As they walked back, the trullo houses came into view, then disappeared just as quickly. 'Who lives there?'

Greg glanced across, then moved her quickly on. 'Just the workers in Makso's fields. Farm workers.'

'They're pretty houses. Where do the children go to school?'

'I don't know.' The house was in sight. He'd got her back safely. As they approached, baby Ivo was crying.

'Poor Ivo.' She looked up towards the

master suite. 'Maybe I'll get to meet Mrs Yurcich today.'

'Maybe.' He punched numbers into the alarm system and edged her over the threshold. 'I won't come in, my boots are dusty. If you need any help at any time, I lodge in the cottage by the pool. Part of my role is maintaining security, so I keep an eye on the grounds. I live over there.' He pointed it out, keen to let her know exactly where to find him. He still wasn't sure where her loyalties lay. Time would tell. 'Have a good breakfast.'

'Thank you. And thanks again for helping.'

'I'll sort the bike out. If you want to go cycling again, don't go alone. Let me know; I like a bit of exercise.'

He watched her go indoors, and hoped she would take up his offer. It wasn't entirely safe out in the fields for a woman alone. He could only do so much on his own, and her being here worried him. Then he set off back to his quarters to look for a bicycle repair kit.

Mel went inside, showered, and dressed. Poor Greg's hanky was a mess: she'd wash it before she gave it back. His kindness touched her. She was just about to go down to breakfast when she went to close the curtains to keep the sun out. Something caught her eye. A rolled-up ball of paper sat on her balcony. She opened the doors and looked around, but all was silent: only the garden lay slumbering under the morning sun.

She picked up the ball. It was heavy. Inside the sheet of simple lined paper was a stone. Someone had thrown this deliberately for her to find.

Curious, she uncrinkled the ball of paper. On it were three simple words which carried a wealth of meaning and sent a shiver down her spine. *PLEASE. HELP. ME.*

2

Mel stared at the note. Who could have sent such a cryptic message? Why had it been thrown to land on her balcony?

She went and scanned the garden, hoping whoever had thrown the message might still be around. The household was beginning to wake, and she needed to be down at breakfast soon. Makso was going to brief her on her duties and he didn't tolerate lateness.

Shielding her eyes from the blinding sun, she cast around. There was no one there apart from Greg Brodie, fixing the bike, surrounded by a paraphernalia of tools. He'd told her part of his role was security. Should she tell him about the note? He had been very solicitous towards her, but she wasn't sure she could trust someone she didn't know.

Suddenly, he looked up at her. The pool was surrounded by trees. It might have been coincidence, but she wondered that he had chosen to be in the one place there was a break in the greenery where he could view her balcony. Mel shot back into her bedroom and drew the curtains. Surely he wasn't watching her …

She was due downstairs in minutes. She grabbed her bag and put in a pad and pen. She wanted to be as efficient as possible. Then her eye alighted on the crumpled-up note on the bed. She mustn't leave it in plain sight. Someone had taken her into their confidence. She went back in, tucked the note in her bag, and hurried downstairs.

She arrived at her seat thirty seconds before Makso strode in. Severina bustled behind him, clanking silver pots in hand. 'Tea?'

'Coffee please.' Mel needed a shot of caffeine to keep her wits about her.

'You slept well?' drawled Makso.

'Like a log.'

'Good. We have a busy day ahead. Some influential friends are visiting this evening, I am hosting a dinner party and I want you there. They're interested in purchasing artworks: some are knowledgeable dealers, others investors. Although I love my treasures dearly, they're all for sale. You will chat to people, encourage them to buy.'

'But … ' Mel wasn't hungry any more. Her stomach felt heavy. 'I know nothing about the art world.'

Makso picked at figs and yoghurt. He obviously lived on his wits rather than a large diet. 'You'll learn. You'll spend today with books from my library, and you will study the artworks I have on display. By this evening I expect you to hold at least a half-competent conversation.'

Mel opened her mouth to protest. This baptism by fire was a test of her worth. His look warned her to keep silent.

She swallowed hard and made herself eat a croissant off the pile. He mustn't know how inadequate she felt. Makso Yurcich was a hard man, but she wanted him to have confidence in her.

'I won't disappoint you.' She shot him a dazzling smile. 'I always loved Art at school, and although it's been a long time, it'll be a pleasure.' She surprised herself, sounding so convincing. 'I presume Mrs Yurcich will be there helping you host the dinner.'

'I have asked Hiroko. But I doubt she will make an appearance. She has not been up to hosting dinner parties lately.'

'Perhaps she and I could get ready together. Young mothers who've spent a lot of time out of the social whirl can find socialising difficult.' Mel had been looking forward to helping Makso's wife. He was absorbed in his business, and not making Hiroko a priority, but Mel would. She'd worked with mothers after childbirth. Helping them get back to their old selves was the best thing for their babies.

Makso stood up. 'Hiroko will appear when she's ready. Severina will show you to the library.' Then he hesitated, appearing to be considering something. 'On second thoughts, perhaps it is a little unfair of me to leave you to your own devices with a pile of turgid books. Come with me to the library, and I will give you a crash course on my most special pieces of art. Then I will select some books which will be of particular use to you.'

After half an hour with him, she felt better-equipped for the task ahead. When he left her, the room was hollow without his presence. He had that startling knack of commanding and dominating a space, like a politician or a professor. Mel had been terrified about tonight, but now she felt fired up for the challenge. She wasn't one to give in.

Four hours later, she'd filled an exercise book with notes. Learning absorbed Mel, but she needed to stretch her legs. A map in the study showed that the village of Vodnjan was only a short distance away. As she went out into the sun, there was Greg Bodie fixing the pool lights.

'Another beautiful day.' He straightened up.

'Yes, gorgeous. I was thinking of having an hour in Vodnjan.'

'That's all you need. D'you want a lift?'

'No thanks, I need the exercise,' she

said, then saw the bike fixed and ready leaning up against the wall. 'Can I take this?'

'There are hills, and it's easier by car.'

'I can cope.' It was as if he was reluctant for her to be independent. She jumped on the bike, giving him a deliberate wave. 'Thanks, I'll take care of it,' she called, cycling off. 'If you don't see me in two hours, send a search party.' Negotiating the gate, she glanced back and saw Greg on his mobile. Funny, considering that before she'd emerged from the house, he'd been thoroughly immersed in fixing the light.

Vodnjan was one of those picturesque hill towns with a main square where everyone gathered. A general store with fruit and veg at its hub, with ladies who spent more time chatting than buying. A Croatian flag fluttered over the sleepy town hall. In the corner was a deserted tourist office. Children ran around launching wind-up toy birds. Laughing, they sent them soaring into the sunshine, then skidding down onto the ancient flagstones. Mel stopped her bike next to the café, the waft of fresh coffee irresistible.

She took a shady table, ordered cappuccino, and watched people meeting and greeting friends. Cats walked, high-tailed, sniffing out tidbits. As she sat, a couple of lads wheeled a trolley bearing bottles of syrupy brown liquid. They gestured her to look, gabbling enthusiastically in their native tongue.

'I'm sorry, I don't know if I want any. What is it?' One of the boys poured a sample in a paper cup for her.

Suddenly the man next to her said, in a rich, deep American voice, 'Bit early in the day, isn't it?'

She'd been too absorbed in the goings-on in the square, but now she looked, she saw a long-legged young man with striking grey eyes. With his cropped beard he looked like a handsome buccaneer. His sky-blue summer suit topped an open-neck shirt so white it hurt her eyes. Not an ordinary tourist, she decided, looking at his leather briefcase; possibly here on business.

'It might be,' she admitted, 'but I don't know what they're trying to sell.'

'It's grappa, the local firewater. They chase it down with coffee. The home-brewed version is great, but only if you like your alcohol to kick like a donkey. It's more powerful than kryptonite.'

The lads showed her the different labels. 'It would be good to have something made in the area to take back. It's difficult to buy nice presents. What's in it?'

'It's a distilled liqueur made from stems, seeds and gunk left over from the grapes after wine production. They flavour it with anything in season.' He pulled his chair closer, examining the labels, and Mel smelt vetiver aftershave on the sun-kissed air. 'This one's flavoured with walnut, that one with sage and honey, and this with berries and leaves of mistletoe.' She sniffed. Pungent alcohol mixed with herbs hit her between the eyes, making her head swim, but she didn't try it. He was right; it was too early.

'Wow, so aromatic. The mistletoe one

would make a lovely Christmas present.' Mel thought of Oscar, her friend and previous employer. He loved unusual liqueurs, and the two young men were eager to make a sale.

'That's a great idea,' said the American. 'I'll get one myself. Shall I bargain with them for a special price for two bottles?'

'Okay.'

Two minutes later, the deal was done. The lads were happy. She gave her new companion her share of the cost, and they shook hands. 'Ryan Peacock, real pleased to meet you.' His West Coast accent was dreamy, his handshake warm and confident. She so hated a limp, non-committal offering; a firm handshake denoted a forthright character. 'Are you staying nearby?'

'I'm working at the Villa Lavanda.'

'Seriously? I'm due there tonight.'

'Are you? What for?'

'I collect art. I don't know Makso Yurcich well, but I'm keen to see his collection. I'll be excited to view Roman silver plate, ceramics by the Impressionists, and Assyrian marble reliefs. He has varied tastes.'

'Well, I'm not looking forward to it!' She blurted out what had been on her mind all morning.

Ryan leant forward, stroking his beard. 'Why not? It sounds a fantastic evening.'

'I'm Makso's new assistant. Very new, and before I came here, I knew little about art. I've spent all morning studying, but I'll be a total fish out of water and won't fool anyone.'

'You're soooo wrong.' Ryan ordered more coffee for them: black, sweet and strong. She listened to his refreshing take on things, and realised she hadn't smiled so much in ages. He had an endearing habit of talking with his hands. 'The art world's full of guys blowing their own trumpets, dudes who love to show how much they know. They wanna impress others. You won't get a word in edgeways. If you get stuck, come on over and talk to me. Go on, tell me what you learned in your studies this morning ... '

As she talked, she was surprised at the

amount she had taken in. They chatted, he interjecting with interesting facts from his extensive knowledge. He had a quirky way of explaining things with little diagrams. In a while, she sat in front of a pile of paper napkins covered with historical timelines and tips from Ryan on how to test the provenance of antiquities. 'Tonight, we'll all be asking Makso about the correspondence or old catalogues which he'll have to go with his artworks, proving they're genuine. Each item will have a story, details of where it's been exhibited, invoices from when and where it was sold. But that's just the business side of art. Most importantly, art should evoke emotion. Which of his pieces d'you like, which d'you hate?'

'Well, he has a beautiful pink alabaster goddess. He told me all about her this morning. She's cold to the touch, and so beautiful.'

They began an involved discussion. 'There,' he said finally, 'you're really getting into your stride because you're expressing your own opinions. You're backing up your views with valid arguments. Be yourself tonight, Mel, and you'll surprise even the great Makso Yurcich.' Ryan sat back, crossing long legs, with the air of a master who had taught an A-star pupil.

'I feel better now, thank you. It's an amazing coincidence bumping into you.'

'Not at all.' He waved his hand at the square. 'Vodnjan's a little place. I've sat here most of the morning and keep seeing the same people. The population's tiny. You're not in London any more, just like I'm not in San Francisco.'

She glanced at her watch. 'Goodness, time's flown. I must get back.'

'And I have places to go and people to see. Hey — ' He shook her hand, holding it a second more than necessary and looking into her eyes. '— look forward to renewing our acquaintance this evening.'

As she cycled away with a light heart, Mel mused on how one person with a positive attitude could turn a day round. Ryan Peacock had given her confidence in herself. What was more, he was very handsome, and she found herself blushing, thinking of the way he'd looked at her.

Cesare Mazotta sat in silence at the desk in his police station office back in Sorrento, Italy. He'd bought a special pad of expensive writing paper. But after trying yet again to pen a letter to Mel, always in his thoughts, he threw it in the bin. The pad was nearly finished and he still hadn't been able to say what was in his heart. How did you tell a girl you loved how much you were hurting, and how much you missed her, without scaring her away? How did you ask to try again without sounding as if you were begging? It was late, and he must work. Later, he resolved. He would try to write later to the girl he had asked to marry him, the girl who had turned him down and inexplicably run away. But for now, he was done in, his emotions frayed. He straightened his tie, and got back to work. Work was the only place he could find solace.

Mel freewheeled out of the square, past coloured shutters brightly reflected in the afternoon sun. The lavender fields marked the edge of Makso's impressive estate. Perfume from the purple flowers lay thick on the afternoon air, and all seemed right with the world — until she drew near the walls of the Villa and heard an unholy commotion. There was barking and shouting, raised voices, and even crying.

She cycled faster. War had broken out at the normally peaceful Villa Lavanda. As she turned the corner, there in the driveway, clutching his arm, was the chauffeur, Ivan. Severina's husband stared daggers at Makso, who stood with a guard dog at his side. Poor Severina wept. Their son Mihovil comforted her, all the while looking warily at the standoff between Makso and his injured father.

Mel skidded to a halt next to Mihovil. In all the upset, the birthmark on the boy's cheek stood out like a red traffic light. 'What's going on?'

'Angry words have been said. My father

has accused Makso of not controlling his dog. It tried to bite him.'

'Oh dear.'

'Papa is hot-headed. He doesn't like Makso. My mother is upset and telling Papa he must be careful. It seems Makso was looking for him, searched everywhere, then heard he had been down by the trulli houses. But Makso's forbidden Papa to go there.'

'Why?'

'I don't know,' sighed Mihovil. 'But Papa stood up for himself and told Makso that even if he is his employer, he won't be answerable to Makso every second of the day. Papa lost his temper and the dog jumped at him.'

'Surely it wasn't Makso's fault.'

'The dog got excited and pulled at the lead unexpectedly when Papa raised his voice.' Mel could see they'd come to a standoff. But she wasn't having men behave worse than children, and poor Severina looked devastated. Her face was ashen, worried they might all lose their jobs.

Mel waded in, despite Makso's stony stare. Talking very slowly because Ivan's English was not good, she said, 'Please, come away. You haven't been injured, have you?'

Her common-sense attitude and calm voice took the heat out of the situation. Makso, seeing someone take Ivan's side, turned without a word and left them to it. Severina stopped crying and calmed her husband down. He wasn't injured, but he'd lost face. Frustration burnt in his raging eyes. He muttered words under his breath as Severina said, 'Thank you,' and led him away.

'Are you ok?' Mel asked Mihovil. She was conscious the boy was unnerved. She lead him to one of the chairs by the pool. He sat down, tight-lipped.

'My father's a proud man. He may be hot-headed, but Makso is all-powerful in this house, and it frustrates my father.'

'Has this sort of thing happened before?'

Mihovil sighed. 'There is difficult history between Makso and my father.'

'What sort of history?'

'Papa hasn't told me everything. But he and Makso were schoolboys together. Once, they were all poor, all equal. But while my father has remained a humble chauffeur, Makso has a better business head. That's why Papa ended up working for him, my mother too, and now me. Papa fears we are under his thumb and can never get away, even if we want to.'

'Your father could work for someone else.'

Mihovil looked wretched. 'I have said this to Papa, but there is not so much work about. We have a nice house on this estate, and it is close to school and my grand-parents. Besides, I feel there is something strange which ties my father to Makso. He wants to break away, but he can't. Makso has a hold over him. He likes to have — how do you English call it? — the upper hand. The worst thing for Papa would be to lose his job. He is desperate for me to not become a chauffeur like him. He wants me to be something grand: a doctor, or a lawyer. While I am studying, he would move mountains to stay here. I'm scared that what happened today may lose us all our place at Villa Lavanda.'

How different Makso was from her last employer: Oscar, whose daughter Izzy she'd cared for in London, had been kindness itself. Although he was a hot-shot lawyer, he didn't need to be macho. Everyone loved Oscar, but around Makso was an air of unease. She wasn't going to kowtow to him. She didn't have as much to lose as Ivan, Severina and Mihovil. It was time someone stood up to the great Makso Yurcich.

'Don't worry, Mihovil. Go and see your father. I'll speak with Makso, put in a good word for your Papa.'

'Would you?' Mihovil's head lifted and he looked bright again.

'Of course. These incidents where people shout and get angry always seem worse at the time. All will be well, don't worry.'

Mel was troubled as she watched the boy walk away, many thoughts going round in her mind. She thought back to the message on her balcony this morning. *PLEASE. HELP. ME.* Was that note from Mihovil, secretly reaching out to someone to get heard? He couldn't burden his parents with his concerns. Young men felt they needed to be strong for their families.

Mihovil was so shy, especially with that birthmark. When she knew him a little better, she might ask him about the note, and see if he would open up and admit to having written it. The Villa Lavanda, peaceful though it appeared, was a hotbed of conflict and divided loyalties.

She thought about Greg Brodie, and couldn't help feeling he was on Makso's side. He must have heard the commotion — his quarters were close by — and yet he hadn't come out to help. She didn't want to take anyone's side, just to get on with her job.

She turned to go back to the study. As she did, she saw a movement towards the top of the house. On a balcony, just for a few seconds stood a small but very beautiful woman. It was the first time Mel had caught sight of Makso's wife. Hiroko Yurcich was like a delicate bird. Slender, around five foot nothing, with a length of jet-black straight hair. Like many oriental women, she moved gracefully, like a leaf floating on a still lake. In a moment, she disappeared.

Hiroko must have heard the argument going on. But she hadn't come down to defend the staff against her husband. Mel gritted her teeth. One thing was for sure, even if Makso wasn't going to introduce them, Mel was going to jolly well go up there and introduce herself. Part of her job was to look after Hiroko and the baby. She couldn't do that if she spent all her time down here. Taking a deep breath, she set off upstairs.

Greg Brodie was livid with himself. He'd heard shouting from inside his small apartment by the pool, but had stopped himself going out. He'd wanted to confront Makso and speak up for Ivan but he couldn't do that could he? He must tread carefully. What's more, he was homesick.

How long all this would take he didn't know, and having Mel Sanderson in the mix wasn't making things easier. She was a feisty girl, but in this situation, having a mind of your own could make problems — for both herself and for him. He still didn't know what she was really doing here.

Greg looked at his watch. If he didn't hurry, he'd miss his appointment at the internet café in Vodnjan. It was difficult keeping under the radar. He dared not use the computer here. There were eyes and ears everywhere, and he must be careful. He needed to discuss Mel with someone. What was she really up to? He must get to know her, win her confidence. And do research into her background. This game of cat and mouse was difficult, but he was an experienced player.

He changed out of his work clothes and into smart jeans and a black t-shirt, just as if he was setting off for one of the bars like he did most late afternoons. It was surprising what you could pick up from the locals once they'd had a little alcohol and their guard was down. 'Act normally,' he thought, 'keep your cool and keep your head down. Patience is all.'

Tiptoeing on the stairs, Mel made her way to Hiroko Yurcich's bedroom. As she approached the door, it suddenly opened. Mel darted into an alcove. A woman dressed in a nurse's uniform came out, holding a tray with an uneaten lunch on it. The woman had a sharp face with a long nose. The nurse went off downstairs. Mel knew she shouldn't have come up unannounced but it was high time she met Hiroko. She wanted to meet her alone, without the overbearing Makso or the nurse present.

'Who is it?' a voice answered her gentle knock.

'My name's Mel. I've come to introduce myself.'

The door opened a crack. 'Does Makso know you're here?'

'Yes, of course,' said Mel, being economical with the truth. Makso knew she was here at the Villa, even if he didn't know she was up here this minute defying him and taking matters into her own hands.

'Come in.'

There in the corner was the most beautiful crib on a stand. White lace and broderie anglaise adorned the basket, a decorative canopy of sheer cotton protected the baby from the breeze at the window. 'Oh, may I look?'

Hiroko pulled aside the snowy blanket. 'You like babies?'

'I absolutely love them, he's a darling.'

'You can pick him up if you want.'

Mel lifted the tiny body scented deliciously of talcum powder, and her heart lurched into her mouth. She wanted to hold the baby tight and never put him down. Just cuddling him aroused all the maternal instincts she had buried the day she'd been told she'd never have children of her own. She inhaled deep, enjoying every sensation. He was priceless, so pretty, so delicate. 'He's gorgeous.'

'His name's Ivo.'

'I know, Makso told me.' Mel stroked

the skin of his forehead, smooth as a butterfly's wing. She rocked him and he gurgled. 'I'm here to help you look after him, Hiroko. Being a new mother can be daunting. I've loads of experience but I don't come at things from a medical point of view. It's all about you and Ivo, you and your darling boy.'

Hiroko looked at Mel, and said nothing. She seemed distant, unconnected. 'The nurse does everything. He is well enough.'

This woman who looked more like a girl stood, hands behind her back. 'You might want to hold Ivo. He needs you, not the nurse.'

'I don't think so.' Hiroko backed away. Mel felt for her. She was in a strange country, without her own mother for comfort and guidance. Mel stepped forward and gave Hiroko her tiny son. He looked up at her, then reached out one little starfish hand and grasped a soft skein of his mother's hair. 'He likes me.'

'Of course. He loves you, you're his mother.'

'I've not taken him out. I haven't been out of the house for weeks.'

'Why not?'

'It's the nurse's job.'

'Nonsense. Let's take him out tomorrow. I'll come and knock for you at 10am.'

'What about the nurse?'

'You're the mistress, and this is your baby.'

She gazed at him, expressionless. She looked like a porcelain figure. Soon Mel could see that the baby was yawning and Hiroko was tiring. If she was having to battle against a domineering nurse she probably needed time on her own. 'Let's put him back in his crib.' As Hiroko placed him down in the crib by the balcony, Mel couldn't help noticing that her own balcony was literally just a stone's throw on the next floor down. Had it been Hiroko who had sent the message this morning? Was it she who had asked for help?

When Mel got downstairs, she felt very alone. It had been a strange day. On the other hand it could have been the gaping hole in her heart. The emptiness of childlessness which had been highlighted by holding baby Ivo so close knowing she would never hold her own baby. Or maybe it was worrying about the note that was still safely tucked in her handbag. When she got to her room she felt like a ship at sea, adrift without an anchor. Who would she have called upon when she was back in Italy staying with her good friends Caroline and Antonio? She knew the answer without thinking. Cesare Mazzotta's kind, clever face formed in her memory. He knew the answer to most things. Besides he was a detective and there were undercurrents in the Villa Lavanda of a mystery that needed solving.

Mel hadn't spoken to him since their broken relationship. But, it was on a professional level she wanted to speak to him now. He could advise her what to do about the note. She dialled his number. There was no reply, it went to voicemail. Should she leave a message, would she sound crazy? Would he even talk to her when she'd turned down his proposal? Instead, she left a brief greeting, trying to sound breezy. 'Hi Cesare, it's Mel. Long time no speak. Wondering how you were, and if you'd like a chat. Perhaps, if you have the time, you could give me a ring.'

She rang off feeling the need for air. Severina had said there was a sun terrace on the roof, from which you could look out to sea. It might be cooler upstairs. Mel went off and sat up there gathering her thoughts for ten minutes. She now felt able to have a bath and get ready for the evening's dinner party. Her thoughts turned to Ryan, the lovely American she had met this morning, and she realised how much she was looking forward to seeing him again. In fact, as she chose a pale green cocktail dress, she knew she was choosing it because he'd said green was his favourite colour. It was too soon after her relationship with Cesare to think about dating, but it was nice to be appreciated.

The time for dinner was almost here and Mel felt hotter than ever, the evening was so steamy. One last trip to the cool roof, to get her courage up would help. She climbed the stairs, opened the door and breathed in the scent of pine trees and sea air blowing in off the coast. The light was failing and she could make out only the outline of trees against the navy-blue sky. As her eyes began to adjust, she peered in the direction of the trulli houses to the secluded inlet. That bit of coastline would surely be deserted and yet she could see lights bobbing on the water. She moved closer and squinted her eyes. What was going on? Was that a truck, kicking up a pile of dust?

She would have liked to take a trip down there and taken a proper look when she heard footsteps, and Greg Bodie emerged from the shadows. He'd been behind one of the chimneys on the roof all the time. 'What the hell are you doing here?' His voice was harsh, he sounded wound up. What's more she caught a glimpse in his hand of binoculars.

I could ask you the same, she thought, but managed to keep her cool. She wanted to get away from him as quickly as possible. 'Just taking the air,' she tried to sound nonchalant before she blurted out, 'sorry I disturbed you. I have to go. I'm expected at dinner.'

She had caught him doing something odd, and she only felt safe when she was back downstairs, away from him. *Oh Cesare*, she thought as she tried to stop her palms sweating. She could feel her stomach filling with butterflies as she went to enter the dining room. I wish you were here with me, *I wish I weren't so thoroughly alone.*

3

Mel took three deep breaths then entered the dining room. Makso gave her a stoney stare and she knew she was being tested, yet again. It felt like she was walking onto a stage spotlight in front of a very unforgiving audience. So many important experts yet she was expected to hold her own and chat to these men. *Stay calm, just listen and nod your head and don't say anything stupid.* She was the only female guest. All Makso's smart, splendid art dealer friends were men, and all of them clad from head to toe in Gucci shoes, Chanel suits and dripping with expensive watches. She felt about as confident as a lamb amongst a pride of hungry lions.

Mel had been completely wrong-footed by the uncomfortable encounter with Greg Bodie on the roof, and her nerves had only just settled. What on earth had he been doing skulking about with binoculars? And what was happening down in the isolated cove on the beach at this time of the evening? Was he involved in some sort of modern-day smuggling? He'd certainly snapped at her in a way that said he was rattled she'd found him there. Mel noticed her arm as she held out her champagne flute to Severina for filling, and saw that it was shaking. She gulped down a mouthful of champagne for Dutch courage. Suddenly she didn't feel a hundred percent safe at the Villa Lavanda.

'Are you ok?' whispered Severina.

'Just a bit nervous,' Mel admitted and it was nice to know she had at least one ally in the room. Then, through the crowd of grey and black suits, a friendly face emerged. It was Ryan Peacock, looking delicious in a smart black jacket and white linen shirt. He held out a hand in greeting with an open genuine smile which warmed her like a sunbeam. 'Mel, how good it is to see you, you look wonderful. Now, come on over and tell me what you think of this.' Typically American, he wasn't shy in coming forward and out of the corner of her eye, Mel saw Makso observing her with a quizzical but not unapproving look.

She was going to make the most of the lovely Ryan's approach which she grasped like a rope thrown to a woman in a sea of sharks. How kind of him not just to make her feel at ease but also to show her boss how she was in fact already acquainted with one of his important guests. True, it was only the slightest of acquaintances, but Ryan clearly wasn't about to let Makso know that.

She gulped, then plucked up the courage to say what she thought of the artwork Ryan had directed her to. 'It's very beautiful in its own way. I love the black clay and the gloss on the figure. It's naive but with a simplicity which says a lot more than many more crafted pieces of the time. It's an aeolipyle isn't it?'

'Yup, they're curious things, little figures filled with water from a small opening near the back designed to be placed close to a fire,' said Ryan.

'And then the water boils and the steam escapes as a constant blast from the small hole in its mouth. They were used in various ancient rites and religious rituals I understand.'

'You got it. A little bit of magic to please the natives.'

'I guess the water might have been scented with myrrh or sandalwood. It must have helped to create an extraordinary atmosphere in a temple, a bit like incense does in churches today.'

'It would go great with my collection. I have many other artefacts from medieval times. Perhaps you could show me the provenance, has it appeared in any auction catalogues?' Ryan was admiring the strange jug, observing it from different angles.

Makso came up to join them, a wide smile on his face. The piece was one of the most expensive in his collection. 'It is for sale, and at a good price for the right buyer. I would want it to go to someone who appreciated it.'

'Oh I would only buy something I really admired myself. It's a curious thing being a dealer, each purchase is a wrench because I only buy things I love while at the same time knowing I'm going to have to let 'em go one day.'

'Don't you keep any of your pieces?' asked Mel.

'Nope, I look on 'em all like children. I love them while they're with me but I have to let them go at some point because there are always more beautiful things to acquire and of course, I have my customers to please. It's like that with us collectors, isn't it, Makso?'

'Of course. We admire things of beauty but in the end it is a business. Thank you for coming Mr Peacock, are you here looking on behalf of a particular buyer?'

'Yes I am. A lady buyer from New York who shall remain anonymous but who can afford the very best. That's why I am so pleased to see you have a lady present tonight, and such a discerning one. I'm very interested to hear which pieces Miss Sanderson recommends.'

Mel felt a rush of heat to her cheeks mixed with gratitude as she heard Makso say, 'then I shall leave you in Ms Sanderson's capable hands, I see another of my guests trying to attract my attention. You must excuse me.' He made a small rigid bow and left.

Ryan beckoned to Severina as she went by with a tray, motioning her to top up their glasses. 'Thank you,' said Mel, 'and thank you for putting me in such a good light with Makso.' Mel hadn't realised that in her anxiousness she had drained her champagne completely. Finally she was beginning to feel relaxed. She even let herself look forward to the rest of the evening. For there was to be a sit-down dinner and she hoped Ryan would stick by her. In fact, he barely left her side as he shepherded her into the grand dining room overlooking the garden. Candelabra crowded with candles quite dazzling the eye had been placed at the long table and in wall sconces. Makso's superb collection of portraits from different ages hung on the wall. He was the perfect host making sure everyone was settled then announcing, 'Severina and her son Mihovil have cooked us some very special Croatian dishes. We will start with the best dressed lobster from Dalmatia, then there is a traditional wine and rabbit goulash served with sauerkraut and artichokes. But please be sure to save some room for the superb honeyed baklava and apple strudla. My friends, raise your glasses and let us begin.'

It was only when the superb meal had finished, and they had adjourned to the lounge for coffee and petit fours, that Mel noticed the door opening a crack and Hiroko creeping into the room like a shadow. Immediately, Mel went over and smiled warmly. 'How lovely to see you Hiroko, can I get you a coffee?'

'Just a small one.' Hiroko's voice was low and she looked down. Mel noticed too how painfully slender she was, the bones sharp in her shoulders. Mel brought over a few of the tempting petit fours to try and encourage her to eat.

'You didn't fancy dinner?'

'I couldn't take all that polite conversation, I am not ready for it yet and I do not know any of these people, they are all strangers and my knowledge of ancient relics is very small. But the smell of coffee tempted me out of my room and Ivo is fast asleep. Stay with me, Mel.'

'Of course I will.'

'I am sad to tell you that we cannot go on our planned walk tomorrow.'

'Why not?'

Mel was sad too. She'd hoped to get to know Hiroko better.

'Makso's parents have invited us over. It is an honour, his father is very rich and has little time but he has made a gap in his schedule. I would rather stay here, but I must go.'

'No worries. We'll do it soon, whenever suits you.'

Mel chatted to Hiroko, trying to make her feel better and even got her to laugh a couple of times. They were debating which of the men might have had a little too much to drink, when a bustling diminutive Japanese man hove into view.

It might do Hiroko good, thought Mel, to chat to one of her own countrymen in their own language for a change and as the gentleman nodded in a friendly manner as he went by, she introduced them. 'Hiroko, this is Mr Taganika, he is from Osaka. Mr Taganika, Mrs Hiroko Yurcich.'

'Konnichiwa,' said the man, bowing politely.

There was a sudden uncomfortable silence while he stayed with his head bent. Hiroko bowed her head too, but no sound came out of her mouth. The man said something else in Japanese and waited expectantly, but still Hiroko didn't speak. In fact it was almost as if Hiroko hadn't understood him. Mel was mystified, she didn't know what to say or do, she felt so bad for Hiroko. Was it just nerves which meant that Makso's wife couldn't even speak to a stranger? Post-natal depression could do strange things to women and in Hiroko's case it seemed it had given her the most crippling social phobia. Suddenly, Mel felt awful for having been the instigator of Hiroko's embarrassment. The poor woman was standing looking for all the world as if she simply wanted to run and hide.

Makso then appeared and put a heavy hand on Hiroko's shoulder. 'My dear, you look tired.'

She looked up giving him a weak smile. 'I fear,' he turned to Mr Taganika, 'it is very hot in here, please excuse us while I take my wife outside, I think she is feeling faint.'

Mel stepped in to save the situation. 'Perhaps Mr Taganika you would like to see some of the Japanese art we have on display.' She steered the gentleman away from Hiroko. She could have kicked herself for exposing her employer's wife to such embarrassment. Nevertheless she did wonder at Hiroko's extreme reaction. She had never seen that in someone with post-natal depression, the poor woman had been dumbstruck. No wonder she didn't come out of her shell much if that was how difficult it was for her. Mel resolved she would find some way of helping Hiroko to overcome her problems.

'You're looking very thoughtful.' She looked up and there was Ryan. 'People are filtering out into the garden to make the most of the night air. Makso's got some folk musicians in playing tamburitzas, they're really very good. Would you like to join me?'

As she and Ryan listened to the music, people went off into huddles, obviously debating the merits and prices of the pieces they had seen that evening and deciding on which ones they might buy. She followed Ryan round the swimming pool and to the edge of the garden where a delectable perfume of lavender hung on the air like a scented mist. Ryan inhaled deeply. 'Well, have you enjoyed the party?'

'In the end, yes.' She couldn't say it, but it was mainly due to him that her evening had been a success instead of an ordeal.

'I wanted to ask you something.'

'I hope it's not about the art works, I've used up just about all my limited knowledge.'

He turned and smiled. He looked so relaxed and handsome in his smart suit, leaning against an olive tree, with his carefully cut beard and those dreamy eyes. 'I'd like to see you again.' She felt her pulse quicken. Surely it was too early after Cesare and she had split up. She hesitated, not knowing what to say. 'Hey, no pressure. It's just it would be nice to have you along to do some sightseeing with. It's a beautiful country, but it's not much fun sightseeing on your own. Have you been to Pula yet? There's a wonderful amphitheatre and a great little market. We could go tomorrow afternoon, after lunch, then stay on for some supper.' He leaned down and plucked a sprig of rosemary, crushing it for the scent and waiting patiently for her answer.

The rosemary was intoxicating, the air still and heavy. Music wafted down through the pine trees, the murmur of voices was low and distant. She thought for a moment then said, 'It just so happens I've been given the day off tomorrow. Makso and Hiroko are taking the baby to visit his parents. I'd love to join you.'

As they walked up back to the garden, she turned to look at the sea. 'Ryan, I saw something earlier ... I just wondered.'

'Mm?'

'Do you know anything about that bay where Makso moors his yacht? It's just there was something going on earlier.'

'Like what?'

'That's just it, I don't know. But there were lights and a couple of boats and people loading things on and off. Why would people be doing that in the dark?'

'Could be fishermen.'

'They didn't look like fishing boats, they were too smart, too modern and anyway why would they be landing fish there? Somewhere there isn't even a proper road, just a dirt track. Surely they'd be unloading stuff in a harbour next to the market and shops.'

He stopped and gave her a concentrated stare. 'This is clearly worrying you. Do you think someone's up to no good?'

Mel's head swirled. That's exactly what she'd thought, though she didn't like to gossip. 'There's another thing. I had a note thrown onto my balcony.'

Ryan stopped in his tracks. He suddenly looked serious, different, all his usual softness had hardened. 'Go on.'

'It's probably nothing. But it said, PLEASE. HELP. ME.'

He rubbed his chin. 'Do you still have it?'

'Yes, but not on me.'

'When we go to Pula tomorrow, bring it with you. I'd like to see it.'

Back at the house, everyone was saying their goodbyes. Makso looked pleased, a broad smile across his face. When the house was finally cleared of guests, he closed the door and turned to Mel.

'Well, that was a very successful evening. I have taken a number of orders and an excellent one in particular from Ryan Peacock. I was surprised to see you know him.'

'I don't really, we simply got chatting at the café in Vodnjan. It's a small place.

We hit it off immediately like you do with some people.'

'True. Well, you did excellently. I am pleased with your work.'

You could have knocked Mel over with a feather. This was praise indeed from a hard man. 'Thank you. I'm tired, I think I'll turn in now.' Then, she remembered. 'Is Hiroko ok?'

In a moment, his good nature dissolved. 'Of course. Do not worry about her. She doesn't get out enough, a day at my parents' tomorrow will do her good.' With that he turned and left Mel to wonder whether that would really be the case.

Mel was at a loose end in the morning. All her paperwork was up to date and with Makso, Hiroko and baby Ivo having made an early start, the house was eerily quiet. The last thing Mel wanted was to stick around the garden and pool to bump into Greg Brodie. She needed some exercise after the heavy meal the night before so decided to put on some flat shoes and enjoy the early morning air. As she negotiated her way round the lavender fields, she found herself drawn inexorably towards the sea, to the little cove and towards the trulli houses.

Greg almost didn't see her leave even though he'd stuck close to the house to keep tabs on her. But as soon as he realised she'd gone, he set off with his binoculars to look for her. Rushing out of the back of the house, he only just caught a flash of her red dress in the fields in the distance and he knew immediately where she'd gone and why. It was annoying she'd run into him last night on the roof. If Mel Sanderson started getting in the way, she could scupper so many carefully laid plans. He set off at a run to follow her route down to the cove. He was careful as he ran, to keep to the grassy undergrowth and not on the dusty path. If she looked back and saw a dust cloud she might guess someone was following her. He still didn't know for sure what she was doing here, and in his position you had to be wary of everybody.

When she reached the tiny pebble

beach, he kept a decent distance away and lay down to observe her, shielded by a myrtle bush. He watched as she approached the locked and shuttered beach house, standing on tiptoes to peer in at the window. Hopefully, she might just content herself with looking in there and not venture further across the rocks. 'Curiosity killed the cat,' he whispered under his breath, willing her not to go any further. But then he saw her step onto the rocks and start climbing up trying to get a look beyond the edges of the cove. She must have got a glimpse last night of the boats' lights drawing near, disappearing for a time then reappearing. Had she guessed about the cave? If she climbed round any more she'd see the mouth of the cave and then they'd be done for. He had to do something to stop her.

Quickly searching around near his hiding place, Greg spotted a rock the size of a large grapefruit. He picked it up and hurled it. He was a good shot, he'd been a rugby player in his teens. The rock scudded past the steep cliff face about ten feet above her head and chipped off a shower of stones and pebbles. At the same time, a huge gull which had been sitting unseen on one of the ledges flew off with a great squawking and clattering of wings. Mel looked up at the bird obviously thinking it had disturbed the rocks. Greg was in luck. As he watched, Mel thought better of exploring any more, obviously fearing a further loosening of the rocks. Shaking the dust out of her hair, she backed off. She stood for a while, looking out to sea at Makso's yacht, the breeze blowing her dress and he was struck by how small she looked in her flat beach shoes, how vulnerable all on her own. She was a problem, that was for sure, and one he had to keep an eye on. He could have really done without a nosey woman on his hands.

With relief he saw her turn around and head back for the Villa Lavanda. At least for today she hadn't caused too much trouble, but it had been a close one. He and his accomplices would have to get moving, they simply couldn't afford to hang around much longer.

It was midday in Sorrento, and Cesare had only his sandwiches to keep him company. He wondered what Mel was doing now, in fact it plagued his days. He could bear it no longer, he had to try her number again.

When she answered, his heart was in his mouth. 'Cesare, is that really you? How lovely to hear from you. I've really missed you.'

Her words were just what he'd hoped to hear. 'Caramia, I have missed you too, a thousand times more, believe me.' Her wonderful English accent made him smile and he could feel his heart race. There was none of the awkwardness he had feared. They caught up on news, chatting about Antonio and Caroline and their wedding plans, and how Mel was getting on in her new job. Then she said something that made him stand up, pacing back and forth on his office mobile.

'Cesare, there's something strange going on here.'

She related to him a secret note thrown on her balcony, nocturnal goings on at the little bay near the Villa Lavanda, and the curious Greg Bodie skulking around on the roof with binoculars. 'I don't know what to make of it, Cesare. It's like a jigsaw puzzle but I only have some of the pieces. I love it here and the job's fantastic, but this place is making me feel on edge, there's definitely something shady going on. It's beginning to freak me out and this morning I couldn't shake off the feeling on my walk that someone was watching me. There wasn't, I stopped and looked back a couple of times and I don't know if I was imagining it, but you've always said sometimes hunches can be right. The only person I feel I can trust is Ryan Peacock.'

Cesare felt a stab of jealousy. Nevertheless, he reasoned, it was not a bad thing that she had made a friend. 'Be careful who you confide in, Mel. But this Ryan sounds as if he might be ok, it is good for you to have acquaintances outside of the Villa Lavanda. If you would like, I can have a word with the local police and see if they have heard of anything strange in the vicinity. I will also get them to check up on this Greg Bodie and on Makso Yurcich. Maybe sometime soon, I might come to visit.' He hesitated. 'But only if you want me to.'

'Of course I would, Cesare. I'd be only too pleased to see you. We are still friends, aren't we?' Cesare suppressed a groan. If only they could be more than friends. He resolved there and then to ask for leave from his superiors and try and find a date he could book to see Mel. He was desperate to ask her straight out why she had broken off their relationship so suddenly. But he couldn't do that over the phone, it had to be face to face.

'Yes, dear Cesare, we are still very much friends.'

When he rang off, he felt much better for having spoken to her. Immediately he opened the door to his office and yelled for his best detective. The young man jumped to attention and ran over. 'Tomasso, come here please, there is some research I would like you to do for me. I need you to check out these two people.' He scribbled the names down on a piece of paper. 'One is an Englishman by the name of Greg Brodie, the other a Croatian. And be careful, tread easily. I don't want either of them to get suspicious ... '

Mihovil was in the garden picking figs off the tree, grading their level of ripeness, and carefully wrapping each one in a piece of tissue paper before setting them in a box. He had been studying at his books for hours so it was a blessed relief to do some outside work. 'Hi Mum,' he called out when he heard Severina's key in the door.

'Hello darling.' She went to him, and he turned his cheek to her, allowing her to kiss it although at his age he didn't think it was cool to kiss your mother back.

'I have something nice for you,' she said as she went to pour them a cold drink. Their house was small and simple but kept immaculately. Severina had sewn cushion covers out of the material used for traditional Croatian national costumes, the bright geometric patterns in yellow, navy blue, orange and pink providing a startling colour palette against the white walls. She brought out home-made lemonade in a big jug clinking with ice, it was hot work up the ladder in the tree. 'Come down.' A broad smile lit up her face. Mihovil downed the refreshing drink in one, sweat trickling down his back and saw her push an envelope in his direction.

'What's this?'

'Take a look inside.'

There was a bundle of notes. His eyes widened. 'What? I don't understand.'

'Makso gave it to me for you.'

'Why?'

'He said you are now nearly grown up, so you should be paid properly for your services. He was very pleased with the dinner you helped me cook.' Mihovil counted the crisp new notes. He couldn't believe how much there was. Up until now, he had helped his parents without thinking of payment simply because they both worked so hard. He'd only ever wanted to do something to thank them for paying for his books and extra tutoring. Makso had given him a few Kunas here and there but nothing like this.

'Surely he didn't mean to put this much in. It is unlike Makso to be so generous.'

'I think he made a lot of money last night, the guests were buying many things and it helped that Mel Sanderson was there. A couple of the older men were flirting with her, drinking a bit too much and digging deep in their pockets. They cannot resist trying to impress a good-looking young woman. She is very pretty, don't you think?'

Mihovil was always so busy, either involved in his studies or helping his parents, he hardly had time to look at women or girls. Besides, why would they ever look at him with his ugly birthmark when they had all the other handsome flawless boys chasing them? One or two had shown an interest, but he was convinced they just felt sorry for him and he couldn't bear that.

'What will you do with the money?' Severina sat and opened one of the dark purple figs, handing half to Mihovil. They sat and crunched the sweet intoxicating flesh and seeds, there was nothing like fruit fresh off the tree.

Mihovil knew exactly what he would do. He had a brochure up in his bedroom which was so well thumbed it was practically falling apart. He had been saving hard for over six months and believed he had at least another six to go. But with this windfall, his dream would come true. 'There is enough here to buy a racing bicycle I have had my eye on for ages. It has twelve gears and is as light as a feather. I can whizz into Pula on it, or Fazana and it has larger wheels and an adult-sized frame. The other boys will be so jealous. My old one is creaky and too small since I have grown.' He could see himself now, racing down the winding country roads and climbing hills with ease instead of having to feel his thighs ache with the effort of powering a bike which had seen too much service. 'Mother, would it be in order for me to write a thank you note to Makso?'

'I don't see why not.' 'Your father has some good writing paper in his desk, use that rather than one of your lined exercise books. You are a young man of business now.'

She looked so proud that Mihovil glowed as he ran off to his father's desk. Ivan was not a learned man, he never read a book and he hardly wrote any letters. That was one of the reasons Mihovil was surprised to see some shreds of writing paper in the bin. Without thinking, he reached down and picked up the torn-up letter which was in his father's handwriting. Ivan was bad at anything to do with words, and often asked Mihovil to read and write things for him. Mihovil pieced the torn sheets together. As he read his father's words, all his hopes and dreams, his happy joyous mood collapsed in the space of a minute.

Dear Makso

It is difficult for me to write this but we have known each other since schooldays so I ask you to show some compassion, perhaps even mercy. Remember how we were good friends at school, though I fear everything has changed now. Time can do strange things to a friendship, as can money. I want you to write off the loan you have given me. I have tried to pay it back but I realise as I grow older and you do not pay me any more that it will be impossible for me ever to be free of my obligation to you. It is a very difficult thing for a man to lose face but I do so every day that loan hangs over me. One day I know Mihovil will do very well, and I was truly grateful for your loan to pay for his education. But knowing I owe so much money, and having the debt grow with each month is giving me sleepless nights every time you mention it.

Above all, I do not want to have to go to the police with what I know but I feel every day the pressure of the loan hanging around my neck like a boulder.

If you write off the debt, I will forget what I know and never tell anyone.

The letter ended there. Clearly his father had not been sure how to end it, or perhaps he had thought better of sending it at all. One thing was certain though, his father was horribly in debt to a ruthless man and it had been all down to Ivan paying for Mihovil's tutoring. Mihovil felt sick. What's more, his father knew something the police would be interested in, but he was not telling. The more Mihovil read the letter the more confused he became. 'Oh my beloved Papa,' he said as he held his head in his hands. 'What have you got mixed up in and how on earth am I going to get you out of it?'

4

Suddenly the figs Mihovil had eaten lay like a brick in his stomach. The sanctuary of his comfy family home was tainted with secrets and discord. His father's tidy workmanlike desk at which he'd always loved to sit felt uncomfortable. He dragged himself up out of the seat. What should he do? What would a good, dutiful son, a responsible citizen of Croatia, a boy who wanted one day to be a lawyer do? Learning that his father and Makso were involved in debts, loans and bad things the police would be interested in hit him hard. What's more, it was all his fault. Sweat trickled down Mihovil's back, heat came in waves not from the summer air, but from his very core. His father had got into this mess to pay for his education. The irony was that if Mihovil ever made the great heights his father was aiming for, one snif of this scandal and both their efforts would turn to dust. Mihovil made his decision.

He would go and confess everything to his mother. Severina was honest, sensible and she loved his father. She would know how to handle this to make everything ok. She made everything right from when he was a child and she bandaged scraped knees to when he was a teenager helping him with homework. He would do the proper thing. His father must be eaten up with keeping his terrible secret, it must keep him awake at night. Mihovil vowed to be strong for both parents.

He would break it to his mother gently so she didn't panic. He chose some words, rehearsed his speech, he was ready. Mihovil balled his fists and marched into the garden.

There was Severina lying on the sunbed under shade of their tumbling orange bougainvillea. His grandmother had given them that plant on the day he was born. It was sturdy and productive just like he tried to be. A curve in the bark was shiny, where his mother was wont to stroke it as she passed by, saying it reminded her of the happiest day of her life, the day they had been granted the gift of a son. Severina hardly ever lay down, always having some task to do around the house. She looked so peaceful, a smile on her face, no doubt delighted with the generous earnings she had handed Mihovil earlier. Hands tucked under her head formed a cushion. Her hair — still thick, glossy and jet black, he noticed — had developed grey streaks. If you forgot those, you could see the face of the girl she had been in her teens. The girl in the photo over the fireplace in the lounge, gazing up at Mihovil's father on their wedding day: happy, fresh-faced eighteen-year-olds.

Mihovil went to speak but the words died on his lips. His news would devastate her. All he would do would be to take the burden of knowledge from his own shoulders and land it squarely on hers. How cruel would that be? What a coward's way out, not to even try to sort the problem before letting her know. That was not the way of a caring son. The letter his father had drafted, the one he had been determined to show Severina, trembled in Mihovil's hold.

Suddenly, she stirred, lifted her wrist to her forehead and yawned. Her kind eyes opened. 'Goodness, I went right off there. What is that paper, Mihovil?'

'Nothing.' He smiled his widest smile, tucking the paper swiftly in his pocket.

'Did you write your letter to Makso?'

'Y–yes, of course.'

The lie stuttered out like a curse.

His throat was dry, as if full of dust. 'And I am off to give it to him right now.' A second lie.

'You're a good son,' she said. 'I must get on and start the washing. It's an excellent drying day. I might even make some new curtains, our old ones are faded and I found some beautiful material very cheap in the market. Life can be so good, don't you think?'

'Yes.' His voice rang hollow. How his world had imploded, how he had changed in only a few minutes and it was all down to evil. Evil spreading like brown rot eating remorselessly through the bud of a white lily. Makso had done something bad, it had led to his father having secrets. Now he, Mihovil, had started lying to his mother. The wrong must be righted, he must get help, but he couldn't involve Severina. If he was to prove his manliness, he would protect his beloved mother. Suddenly, he desperately needed the help of his friends, and of one friend in particular. He thought of a pair of thoughtful olive-green eyes and hair which fell like a waterfall over tanned shoulders. He could confide in his friend Ildie, she'd know what to do. 'I'll see you later.'

'All right my son, be back in time for dinner.'

But Mihovil was gone. Had leapt on his bike and was pedalling off towards the square in Vodnjan like a boy possessed.

Previously Mel had only passed through Pula on her way from the airport. Now, she sat in an open-topped hire car being expertly steered by Ryan Peacock.

The breeze as they sped down the road blew her hair, fields of corn baking under the sun flashed by. Ryan secured Ray Bans on the bridge of his nose and said, 'Let's go to the market first and pick up some lunch. Can you cope with fruit, bread and cheese? We'll have dinner later.'

'That sounds lovely.'

'Hey, let's make it a picnic, it's too lovely to sit inside in a restaurant. D'you fancy taking our stuff over and sitting on the harbour wall by the sea?' She was so happy, energised by his positivity. It was a welcome break from all the things troubling her. They walked into the cool of the covered market with its wondrous wall tiles depicting Roman maidens carrying pitchers of wine and baskets of oranges. The scent of the sea, squid and fish of all shapes and sizes teased the senses as their scales shone silver-bright on dripping iced slabs. Bread, cheese, meat, bunches of flowers lush and fresh surrounded them.

'This paski sir ewes' milk cheese is the best, it crumbles and melts in the mouth, want to try some?' Ryan's enthusiasm bubbled over as he filled their bag with Mediterranean crescent rolls scented with rosemary, basil and thyme. Outside were stalls under gay red umbrellas, each owned by ladies down from the hills to sell produce from their stallholdings. They beckoned and grinned, skin tanned the colour of walnut oil. Their stalls were proudly displayed with fruits the colour of a Croatian sunset, cherries, peaches, nectarines.

Another stall had Mel trying to converse with the stallholder to find out what the curiosities piled on it were. 'It seems they're white peppers and orange beetroots,' she told Ryan after much gesticulating and giggling from the ladies.

Then there was one with honey in all varieties from the foothills and the plains. White labels on little wooden sticks proclaimed the flavours, castagna, fiori — chestnut, flowers. Ryan bought her a small jar made from bees fed on lavender, sweetest honey for the 'sweetest girl to have with her breakfast yoghurt'.

Was he flirting with her? Mel blushed the colour of the pinkest sweet williams on the corner stall.

Mel and Ryan sat on the harbour wall, feet dangling over crystal water. While they ate, they fed crumbs of bread and cheese into the waiting fish's mouths. The fish made gulping sounds on the surface of the calm sea like sloppy kisses.

When they were full, Ryan gathered up their things. 'The amphitheatre's lovely if you fancy a look.' He held out his hand to help Mel up and she took it willingly. It was firm and dry making her feel safe as he half lifted her to a stand. They laughed as the breeze caught her full cotton skirt making its orange and yellow butterfly patterns dance.

'Shall we go to the amphitheatre now?'

'Of course.'

She wondered whether he might keep hold of her hand, but he let it fall back to sit unheld at her side. They wandered for a while across the amphitheatre's oval space, thinking their own thoughts. Of the countless souls who had lost their lives there. Of the tiny dramas of love and passion played out by the ancient Romans who centuries ago would have shopped in the Istrian markets just like they had done, and where boys had stolen first kisses from cherry-flavoured lips.

Ryan looked up at the walls with their arches. 'Don't the pale limestone bricks look cool against the blue of the sky?'

Not as blue-grey as your eyes look when the sun's in them, thought Mel unable to take her gaze from him. 'See those slabs up there,' he pointed, 'that's where the Romans fastened a canopy to protect the spectators from the sun. Can you imagine the deafening roar from a crowd of 20,000 people watching gladiators fight?'

'I'm glad they don't have fights today.'

'Ah, but they do have reenactments, in full costume, that must be a thing to see.' Ryan turned round and round, his arms spread as if acknowledging an invisible toga-wearing crowd, then made himself dizzy and laughed as he tottered and pretended to be falling so she had to grasp him. Mel liked a man with a sense of humour. She was startled by the strength of his muscles through his summer jacket as she made to catch him. His beard had tints of copper in the sun. For a fraction of a second she wondered how soft it might be brushing against her cheek.

A toddler had separated from her family. Running by, she tripped on a tuft of grass. Ryan righted her as if she were no heavier than a fallen skittle then turned her to run back to her mother. Would Ryan be a man who wanted children? Somehow Mel thought not, as she watched him forget the child and turn back to his guidebook. He was well read and well travelled, she couldn't imagine him wanting to curtail his career having children.

'This amphitheatre isn't as elaborate as the Colosseum in Rome but I kinda prefer it, it's neat. It's perfectly sited here with the breezes off the sea. Now here's a thing, Wembley Stadium is based on the original Colosseum, ain't that amazing?

That we're still designing buildings to the specification of the ancient Romans. Those guys sure knew engineering.'

Being unable to have children, Mel couldn't help feeling a partner who had other interests would be ideal, even if he did spend half his life travelling the world looking for artworks. Ryan was a universe away from Cesare, who was shorter and stockier. Cesare wore his hair shorn and his chin clean shaven whereas Ryan had a wealth of hair and a dashing beard. Cesare was always caring, sometimes serious and a total romantic. Ryan was fun and breezy and didn't worry about a thing. Even now, he was chatting about chariot racing and superheroes from American comics. The two men were chalk and cheese and Mel felt her heart in a ping pong match weighing up the two of them. She wanted Cesare but he wanted children. Ryan had told her how pretty she was and asked her out but he spent his life globetrotting.

They left the amphitheatre and had begun strolling any which way.

'You're very deep in thought, young lady,' said Ryan.

'Oh I'm sorry, I was just thinking.'

'Of what?' They wandered through the triumphal Arch of Sergius into the tightly packed streets of the old town. People with shopping bags hurrying to and fro, tourists dawdling. Now his tone was serious. 'Were you thinking about the note that was thrown onto your balcony?'

'Oh yes.' In fact Mel had forgotten all about it, she was so enjoying herself. She dug deep into her bag, handing the note to Ryan.

'Hmm. It is strange, and worrying. Have you shown this to anyone else?'

'No.'

He rubbed his beard, and nodded. 'There is something I could do. I have a friend, now don't laugh, but he's a private investigator, a good old-fashioned PI Joshua helped me once find a lady who bought some valuable paintings off me then did a moonlight flit without paying. I couldn't get my money and it looked as if I was going to lose thousands of dollars. Took him a while to find her but he did. Not only did he get the paintings back all in one piece, but she was indicted for fraud. Had a string of convictions. Joshua's a good guy. Just so happens he's holidaying this way with his wife Kaylee, they're stopping off on a cruise ship at Rovinj tomorrow. Would you like me to show him the note? His ship docks at 10 am, I can get the note to him and he can do a bit of detective work on it. He's big on fingerprinting and forensic evidence. Never goes anywhere without his little flight case of dusting powder and brushes. He's got chemicals in there that can test for saliva, blood, anything.'

'I don't think he'll need anything like that.' Mel was alarmed. 'Nothing ghastly's happened to anyone at the Villa Lavanda.' Then Mel thought back to Makso's dog which had attacked Mihovil's father Ivan. She shook the thought out of her mind. That was just an accident.

'Sorry Mel, I didn't want to frighten you. I let my imagination run away with me. Watching too many *CSI* programmes can do that. But hey, my friend'll be in Istria all day. Rovinj's a lovely place. If you fancy it, we could meet him for drinks in the afternoon before his ship leaves, and he can tell us his opinion. What d'you reckon?'

He took her hand in his and a thrill raced up through her fingers, into her chest and ended somewhere in the depths of her tummy. How could she resist? 'Okay. It has been worrying me.'

'Attagirl.' Just one thing.' He continued to hold her hand. 'There's no point testing for fingerprints if he has nothing to go on as far as the other people in the house are concerned. He'd need to eliminate people like Makso, Severina, Mihovil, and Ivan and maybe even Hiroko. It would be awful if that were Makso's wife who was so unhappy. It's a real easy thing to collect fingerprints, you could do it. You just have to have something the person's handled. A can of drink, a glass or cup, even a book with a plastic cover. If you were able to bring a few items like that along, we could eliminate people. What d'you think. It'd be fun.'

'Wouldn't it be snooping?'

'Nah. It'd be like we were in an Agatha Christie novel or something. It'd be assisting. That note's a desperate call for help, don't you want to help the poor person who wrote it?'

'Well, of course I do but – .'

'Then let's do it. No one would know, and you'd be back at the Villa as soon as we'd finished drinks with Joshua and Kaylee.'

Before she knew it, she'd been swept along by Ryan's energy and had found herself agreeing to his unorthodox plan.

The sun was waning, but the air was as warm as soup when Ryan dropped Mel off at the Villa Lavanda. During the ride, he'd chatted about her 'mission' as he called it to collect the fingerprints and as with everything with Ryan, he turned it all into a game. 'See how many you can come up with, as many as possible would be good. I've got to go into Rovinj real early tomorrow to see some clients, I'll drop round to the Villa first thing and wait outside about eight-ish. Just put the things in a carrier and bring them out, I'll be there. I won't ring on the bell, I don't want to wake up the whole house. Then I'll pick you up after lunch and we'll pop into Rovinj together to see Joshua. You're sure you can get the afternoon off?'

'Yes, Makso and Hiroko are taking Ivo to the doctors to get his jabs. The doctor's a personal friend of Makso so they've been invited for a long lunch. I've got a load of paperwork to do but I get terrible insomnia so I'll get stuff done by staying up late this evening. Perhaps that'll make me tired enough to help me get a good night's sleep.'

'Well, g'bye then.' Ryan leapt back into his car and sped away. She had hoped he might want to hold her hand, or to give her a peck on the cheek, but perhaps he wasn't keen on her in that way after all. Men were so difficult to read.

Lost in her own thoughts, Mel opened the gates of the Villa Lavanda and walking round to the pool, encountered Greg. He was on a ladder pruning one of the albizzia trees. She hadn't seen him since their uncomfortable clash on the roof the other night and she still wasn't sure about him. His shorts were soaked in sweat which had poured down his back, he certainly worked hard. But what had he been doing on the roof that night spying with binoculars?

As soon as he saw her, he climbed down the ladder. As he did, she noticed a can of coke he had been drinking, discarded on the path. It occurred to her that Greg could possibly have written that strange note. Was he into something dodgy and wanting help to get out of it? She tried to keep an open mind. You couldn't always tell a book by its cover, and he had helped her fend off that snake shortly after she arrived. Mel didn't like to think ill of anybody and she now wanted to get hold of Greg's drinks can as part of her investigations. It must be full of his prints. She had never considered Greg as writer of the note. She felt like a younger version of Miss Marple, and one thing she did know was that you had to engage people in conversation if you wanted to know what they were up to.

'That tree looks super, much neater than before.'

'Thank you.' Greg wiped his forehead, bent down and drank from the can. Then, he surprised her by saying, 'Look, I've been trying to catch you for a word. I'm sorry I snapped at you the other night.'

'That's alright. I'm sure you had your reasons.'

'Makso's been worried lately, there've been break-ins at houses in this area. He thinks it's a gang of itinerant Italians, it's easy for them to come over under cover of night, do a few burglaries then take off. He was worried about his yacht, and he puts me under pressure all the time, do this, do that. I need this job, I have a wife and baby at home. I haven't told anybody here. If I revealed that to Severina or Ivan they'd keep on asking about them. My wife relies on my wages, so I have no alternative but to do everything Makso asks and to be sharp about it. Being under pressure makes me short-tempered.'

'I'm glad you told me.'

'Friends?' He took off his glove and held out his hand.

'Friends.' She shook it. That explained why he was so often on his phone. How sad was that that he'd had to leave his child.

'How old is your baby?'

'Huh?'

'The baby, how old is it, is it a girl or a boy?'

He hesitated. She saw him gulp. He looked at the can and drained it. He seemed lost for words. Goodness, she'd hit a raw spot. 'Um, a year now, she's a year that's it.'

'I won't ask you any more, I can see how upsetting it is. Sorry I pried. Look, you've got such a pile of cuttings here, and it's still boiling hot, what can I do to help?'

'Nothing.' He seemed to have recovered. 'It's ok, I'm nearly done, then I'm going off into Vodnjan to drown my sorrows. I like to prop up the bar and imagine I'm back home in a real English pub.'

'The least I can do is take that can from you, I'll throw it in the bin on my way in.'

'Okay.' He shrugged his shoulders and handed her the can. She took it gingerly by the rim so as not to spoil any prints. It wouldn't surprise her now to learn that Greg had written that mysterious note calling for help. Maybe she could get him a raise from Makso. If she could do that, she thought wandering away and sending Greg a friendly wave as she went, she'd be a miracle worker.

Mihovil propped his bike up against the side of the town hall. There was his group of friends, fellow students, gathered together as always at this time of evening joshing and chatting by the benches next to the park. It was one special friend he looked for, as always. Ildie's long curly hair reached down to her waist. There she stood with her back to him. She had in a yellow ribbon today, threaded through her plait in a way that fascinated him. This evening she wore the cutest of dresses, a new one, just above the knee, fitted over her delicate shoulders, falling away like a smock. It glowed white in the sunset.

As always, he tried not to stare and he felt the birthmark on his cheek throb, or so it seemed to him. One of his friends nudged her and she turned. As she looked in his direction, he raised his hand instinctively to hide the port wine stain, and smiled. He knew she wasn't interested in him in that way, she was too shy. Besides, no girls were interested in him in that way, he thought sadly as he looked at his other friends, their hands casually draped around their girls' waists.

'Hi Mihovil.'

'Hi Ildie, how are you?'

'I'm good. Is there something wrong Mihovil?'

'Not really.'

'You look, I don't know, you don't look yourself.' Gently she took his arm and steered him away from the group. 'It's so hot, let's go and sit by the fountain.'

Ildie was the caring one of the group. The one they all brought their problems to: with their studying; with their parents; with each other. She was the shoulder to cry on, the sound of reason and good judgement. Those soulful eyes could take on a thousand problems. It was hardly surprising she longed to be a doctor, and she'd make it. Mihovil knew she would, she was so clever.

'Is everything ok?'

'Actually, I do have something on my mind.'

She tilted her head. He thought she was going to take his hand, he wished with all his heart that she would, but that was never going to happen. Instead he sat on his hands. This was so difficult. 'It's … it's about my father. He's got himself into a horrendous mess. Oh Ildie, I don't know what to do for the best.'

'Tell me about it. You're always helping me with my problems. Maybe I can help with yours.'

Cesare had finished lunch, a perfect dish of ravioli stuffed with hazlenuts nestled in a parmesan and cream sauce. When his best young detective, Tomasso, came into the Sorrento bar and sought him out, Cesare shook his hand warmly. 'I knew you'd be here Commissario.'

'No better place to be at lunch time.' Cesare wiped his lips with his napkin. 'You have found out something useful for me?'

'Yes.' Cesare ordered them both espressos. 'You asked me to investigate Makso Yurcich, the American Ryan Peacock and the Englishman Greg Bodie. I have made some very interesting discoveries. There is a lot going on at the Villa Lavanda, not all of it very savoury.'

'Tell me more.'

'I can find no record of a Greg Bodie living in Southampton. None of the shipyards have had him signed on as a welder or anything else. He is the original man of mystery.'

Cesare rubbed his hand across his forehead. 'And Mel is living practically in the same house as him. That is very worrying. Are you sure, have you double checked?'

'Of course. You have always told me I am too thorough but I cannot help it. I have a contact in Interpol, we were at police college together. I've asked her to run his image and what little we know through their computers, strictly off the record you understand. But I get a bad feeling about him.'

'And Makso Yurcich?'

'He seems above board. The land he farms was owned by an aunt who left it all to him in her will. It had fallen into disuse, he seems to have turned it around in record time. He has transformed barren stony ground into fertile money-making olives and is talking about a factory to process the lavender oil himself into soaps and toiletries. He is quietly growing an empire. He is known not to suffer fools gladly and he knows who to cultivate in local politics. Apparently he is a tough negotiator and many people do not like him but that's often the way in business.

He is the sort of person who is shaking the lazy government officials who were used to a regime which meant they could sit on their behinds all day and achieve nothing. We could do with more of his type round here.'

'Hmm, and Ryan Peacock?'

'I am waiting to hear back on him. My American contact was tied up on a big drugs case but he has promised me something shortly.'

Cesare patted Tomasso on the back. 'You've done well.' He grasped his jacket off the chair and was in too much of a hurry to put it on. 'I cannot let Mel stay there another moment in the company of a man like Greg Bodie without going over to Croatia to find out what's really going on.'

'But Commissario, isn't that a bit of an over-reaction? At least let me find out more about Ryan Peacock before you set off. I'm expecting something by tomorrow.'

'Maybe.' Cesare was torn. He didn't want to alarm Mel by turning up on her doorstep unannounced. He also didn't want to worry her by phoning him with her suspicions before he got there. She was alone enough as it was. He wasn't a man to sit around though and in a second his mind was made up. 'I am off to the Hotel Girasole to see Caroline and Antonio. I will be back later. If you hear anything more radio me straight away.'

Cesare's car sped round the hairpin bends, the Bay of Naples glistening below as his car rose higher in the hills towards Caroline and Antonio's hotel. When he got there, they were holding an introductory drink for a group of Canadians in the hotel foyer. Cesare paced up and down, thinking, thinking, always thinking. As soon as they were free, they came over and kissed him on both cheeks, the continental way. 'Can we go into your office, Antonio?'

'Of course. You look worried, Cesare. What's up?'

He told them everything. 'So, you see, I must go over to see Mel immediately. I have lots of leave due to me but I need an excuse so I don't cause her any upset. I know she loves her job out there and my suspicions could be unfounded but I get the feeling that the Villa Lavanda is like an iceberg with only the uppermost tip exposed. So much more is going on there and I want to check she is safe.'

'Then you're lucky,' said Caroline. 'I was going to phone Mel to say I wanted to go over soon. We've talked together about the fact I haven't chosen my wedding dress. I simply haven't had time and without her to confide in I'm really not sure which of the designs I've seen would be good. I'm in a total quandary. I can just as easily commission my dress from a Croatian dressmaker as an Italian one and it may well be cheaper. What's more, Antonio and I have been talking about him needing a break. All this wedding preparation's exhausted you, hasn't it, darling? All we need to do is let Mel know we're coming over and you can come too. Didn't you say you wanted to see her again?'

They consulted calendars and Cesare

was commissioned to phone Mel and let her know the good news. Instantly he felt better and went back to the police station with a lighter step.

Mel had collected all the fingerprinted items and had them in her carrier bag. She'd managed to squirrel away a teacup Severina had used. Getting Makso's prints was easy; she just took one of the artbooks from his study. Ivan had left one of his Bic lighters in the kitchen and Mihovil had been drinking a takeaway coke when he came in in the evening and had tossed it in the bin before leaving for home. Mel felt clandestine and sneaky when she took it out but was pleased she had evidence on everyone. She'd labelled the things up in her room, taking care not to rub off any prints. For final good measure she put her own fingerprints on a discarded yoghurt carton and put them in the bag. She was just about to leave her room nice and early to go and wait for Ryan when her phone rang.

'Hello?'

'Hi, Cesare! How lovely to hear from you, thank you for phoning.'

'I am sorry to ring this early in the morning but I wanted to catch you in, and tell you the good news.'

'What's that?'

'We are coming over to see you, Mel. Me, Caroline and Antonio, all three of us. Caroline wants to shop for wedding dresses and I . . . '

'Yes?'

'You see I just need to see you, Mel. I've missed you and I want us to talk things through.'

'Things?'

Her legs felt funny underneath her so Mel sat on the bed. Just as well she had.

'Yes. I need to know, Mel, I really need to know, and we will talk about it face to face when I get there. But, I need to know why you turned me down. The real reason why you refused my proposal of marriage.'

5

Mel had showered and dressed ready to go to Rovinj. As she was drying her hair, she suddenly heard a clunk on the balcony. She put down the dryer, looked out, and there, as plain as day, was a large pebble tied with a second note. She would have rushed down there and then to see who had thrown it. But all she had wrapped round her was a towel. By the time she'd put something decent on and got round to the back of the house, the person would have been long gone. 'Hello, hello, is there anybody there?' She didn't want to shout loudly and worry whoever was trying to communicate with her, especially if it was Hiroko who was always as shy and silent as a mouse. But then it couldn't be her, could it? Mel remembered she was out with Makso.

Mel peered into the trees and shrubs. Everything lay still and silent under the baking sun. She picked the note up and read, 'WEDNESDAY EVENING AT DUSK, BY THE TRULLI HOUSES. TAKE CARE, THERE IS DANGER.' She turned it over, but that was it. The note didn't make much sense. What was going on at the trulli houses? She wanted answers, she must go. She needed to share the information with someone. She decided then and there, the only person she would tell would be Ryan. He had become her confidante, dependable, always looking out for her, and she was off to see him now. He'd know what to do for sure. She would have chosen Cesare, but he was not here on the ground where it was all happening. He'd be visiting soon, but for now Ryan was her trusted friend.

Mel took the bus to Rovinj. It was like entering another world. The cobbled streets were so narrow, built in medieval times she guessed, some of them barely wide enough for a horse and small cart. They twisted and turned delightfully. Terracotta roofs bent into each other like old ladies, foreheads touching, sharing secrets. Peeling sand-coloured walls were dotted with shutters. Their shades of sky blue, mustard yellow and racing green lit the town with colour. Above her head assorted washing, vests, shorts and pillowcases waved in greeting like gaily coloured bunting.

Mel hurried to the harbour to meet Ryan. As she did, she passed arched steps going steeply down to the sea. From her guidebook she'd read Rovinj was once an island. These steps lead to delivery points where boats bobbed up against the houses bringing supplies direct to cellars nestling above the waves. Centuries ago, these shops would have sold oils, olives, perfumes, rich fabrics and medieval cures. This was still a place of bustling commerce. Its trade now though was jewellery and trendy driftwood art for cruise ship passengers.

Ryan was waiting at a bar on the quayside, coffee in hand. He got up and waved, looking so pleased to see her, it made her heart soar. 'My you look gorgeous hun, white is definitely your colour and you're getting a tan, it suits you.'

Mel blushed. She'd been brought up in a strict family, where hard work and serious application were the name of the game. She'd never heard her father compliment her mother's green-eyed beauty though he often complimented her on how spick and span she kept the house. Mel was a feisty independent woman yet it didn't stop her glowing to hear she was appreciated for her looks especially with her biological clock ticking fast. In her days as a nanny, most of her acquaintances were female so any attention was a new and welcome departure for her.

'Whad'ya think of Rovinj, cute isn't it?'

'Absolutely beautiful.'

He dusted off a seat for her. 'It's one of the great seafaring ports. Pilots from here were renowned experts in escorting ships to the Venice lagoon. It's still a proper fishing port. That fine-looking ship over there is *The Pride*'. He pointed to a smart cruise liner, its many windows twinkling in the sun. 'Any minute now,

Joshua and Kaylee will be coming down those steps to join us for coffee. Kaylee spent the morning shopping in Rovinj and then had to go back to the ship for a nap. I dropped the fingerprinted things off to Joshua as soon as you gave them to me this morning. He'll have been in his element.'

Mel was desperate to show Ryan the new note and chat about what it meant. But something made her hold back. Kaylee and Joshua were strangers, an unknown quantity. Besides, Ryan hadn't seen his friends in a while and she didn't want to dominate the conversation.

'I feel bad,' she said, 'Joshua shouldn't have spent part of his holiday working to sort out my problems.'

'Oh don't feel bad. The guy's addicted to his work. Believe me, he jumped at the chance to avoid more shopping. He's seen enough medieval Croatian towns to last him a lifetime. Hopefully he'll have some news on who penned that note thrown to you.' A couple appeared at the top of the gangplank and immediately started waving at Ryan, making a beeline for him.

Kaylee was a flawlessly presented woman with clipped blonde hair and shocking pink gel nails. 'How utterly lovely to meet you,' She looked like an advert in Vogue. Taking off her Ray-Ban sunglasses she gave Mel the sort of smile and warm hug a sister might on greeting a brother's new fiancée. A glistening sapphire ring twinkled on Kaylee's finger. 'I love this place, we've sure seen some fabulous sights in Croatia.'

Joshua slapped Ryan on the back and gathered him into a bear hug. Cappuccinos were ordered all round. After some chat about the weather being as hot as Southern California, they got down to the serious business of the fingerprints. 'So whose are they on the note?' Ryan asked.

'Well, it was an interesting conundrum for me,' said Joshua. 'You sure presented me with a variation of different surfaces, a real challenge. Paper isn't the easiest surface to detect fingerprints on. But I use a small quantity of silver nitrate.

Y'see silver chloride turns black in light. When we sweat, as we do all the time, particularly in a hot country or when we're under stress, as your person may well have been when they wrote the note, we produce sodium chloride. I applied silver nitrate mixed with a little distilled water. When the note was exposed to light the print turned black, *et voila*,' he said with a flourish, like a magician explaining a trick, 'the writer's identity is exposed.'

'And,' Mel was on the edge of her seat, 'whose print was it?'

'It belongs to Severina.'

'Severina?'

Of all the people Mel could have imagined, Severina wasn't the one she had put near the top of the list. She'd been convinced it was Mihovil or Hiroko as the two people in the household with the least power, the ones most likely to need help. Severina, the consummate housekeeper, always looked calm, collected and together. What on earth should Mel do with the information now she had it? She hadn't thought that puzzle through.

Could she tackle Severina directly and risk embarrassing her or worse still having her clam up once she was challenged? Clearly though, Makso's housekeeper needed Mel's help, but what help and why? Mel was baffled.

All the while Joshua had been talking, the light had grown more mellow in the late afternoon. Kaylee took off her Ray-Bans and left them on the table. 'We can't stay till the evening, our boat sails shortly. We're off to Italy, won't that be fun? But perhaps we can chat more about what's been going on at the Villa. You look troubled, Mel.'

Mel appreciated the kind gesture. She talked about Severina, Ivan, the attack by Makso's dog and the obvious tension between him and Ivan. It gave her a chance to think things through.

'Sweetheart, you need to tread carefully. I'd say just do your job and don't put your head above the parapet. If Severina needs someone she knows where to find you. You don't want to lose your position at the Villa and this Makso sounds like a piece of work.'

'The only thing I can say,' piped up Joshua, 'from all my years as a private investigator is that sometimes, doing nothing is a perfectly reasonable option. You need to know when to make a move, when to push things forward. But at other times, you need to know when to sit back and wait for things to reveal themselves. If Severina's in any real danger, she'll feel free to speak to you in her own good time. She knows while you're there, she's not alone. It might be better to just to keep an eye things from a distance but stay her friend.'

'That's right,' agreed Kaylee. 'We gals need our girlfriends.'

It was sage advice and as Mel and Ryan waved goodbye to the two Americans, leaving them heading for the ship, Ryan pulled her away. 'Come on, let's take a proper look around Rovinj, we can go up the hill and take in the view. Besides, it'll take your mind off things. Perhaps you need a rest from thinking about all that stuff.'

But Mel wasn't so sure. She was trying to digest the news they had imparted and decide on the best time to mention the new note to Ryan. She desperately wanted to go to the trulli houses on Wednesday as the new note had beckoned her, but if she told him, Ryan might try to warn her off going. She could have told the local police. Only thing was, if it was just some domestic quarrel between Makso and Ivan that had upset Severina, and Mel involved the police, she could lose her job. Her mind was a jumble, so many decisions, so many different paths to take.

Although Mel and Ryan had a lovely walk up the hill, in and out of the shops, Severina was constantly at the back of her mind. The only moment Mel relaxed was when Ryan presented her with a pair of turquoise earrings. 'They're beautiful, you shouldn't have.'

He winked. 'I snuck back to that shop while you were looking at all the sarongs. I could see how taken you were with those earrings, so I couldn't resist. Here try 'em, I'd love to see them on you.' With a deft touch, he helped her when she found the butterfly clips fiddly. As he did so, his hand touched her neck. His expensive cologne filled the air, an intoxicating mix of lime, basil and mandarin. The closeness of him made her dizzy. Even though they were in a crowd, it was as if for those few blissful seconds, they were in their own private bubble. He spoke quietly. 'Oh my those look fine, they're superb against your dark hair. You're a very pretty lady Melanie.' He nodded then looked away, the only time she'd known him to be shy. It sent a flurry of butterflies through her tummy and brought a lump to her throat.

In a short while, Cesare would be visiting, together with Mel and Antonio. She didn't know when yet, he was always so busy it was difficult for him to get time off. But with Ryan being so attentive, it was literally as if her heart was divided down the middle, one half belonging to Cesare, the other reserved for Ryan.

They strolled back down the streets. Mel so wanted to hold Ryan's hand, she was on the verge of making the bold move of slipping her own into his unbidden. But then she was distracted, a lady wandered by with a babe across her middle in one of those slings. He was fast asleep, and his father lovingly adjusted his sun hat. Mel noticed Ryan looking at the pair. 'Isn't that baby sweet?' she remarked.

'Yeah they're cute as anything at that age, but when they grow up, they can be a total handful. I'm the eldest of five and I spent enough of my teens looking after little kids. I reckon I've had my fair share of diapers and bottles. I couldn't wait to get away to college and travel the world. Kids aren't on my agenda, no way.'

Ryan stepped firmly away. So that confirmed it. He was the complete opposite to Cesare. Ryan didn't want children. He would make a woman like Mel an ideal husband. She could feel herself well up. She'd despaired of any man being happy with a girl who was barren, sterile, unproductive, infertile, unfruitful.

There, she'd permitted those blunt words, words she never allowed herself to think of, to crowd into her head. But letting them in, strolling next to a man for whom they carried no power was gloriously liberating. If only she could share those thoughts with Ryan, how wonderful would that be? To hear him say, 'y'know Mel, it just doesn't matter, I've never wanted kids and I never will,' would have freed her. She looked at his hand again, held empty by his side. But she wanted him to make the move. She needed that confirmation from him. Her heart was still so fragile after the break up with Cesare.

Nevertheless, just being near Ryan this afternoon had filled her with happiness. She decided to forget the mysteries at the Villa Lavanda and enjoy the moment. Everything here in this fairytale town was perfect, the colours vivid, the sounds of the birds entrancing. T he faces of people smiling, happy on holiday, came and went as they strolled along. It felt as if everyone were sharing in her feeling of ... hope. That was it. For the first time, hope had bubbled up that one day she would be happily partnered with a good man, and she allowed that hope to grow and flourish suffusing her with a sublime joy. Mel didn't know whether to laugh or cry but it didn't matter, she was floating on air.

After walking their feet off, Mel and Ryan finally ended up at the original café where they'd had coffee earlier. The cruise ship was long departed. 'I just need to use their restrooms, please excuse me,' said Ryan and he left her sitting with a glass of chilled Pinot Grigio at the café.

Now would be a good time to show him the second note. She took it out of her handbag and spread it on the table ready for his return, when suddenly a waitresses came up to her brandishing an item in her hand. In a broken accent she said, 'Miss, I am so pleased you come back. Your friend, she leave her expensive sunglasses, please you give them back to her when you next see her.'

'Thank you.' Mel took them, thinking of the kindly Kaylee, but then said. 'Oh but I can't get them back to my friend. She boarded the cruise ship, she's going on to Italy I think.'

'What, the lady with the sunglasses?' The waitress looked perplexed. 'But she and her man friend do not go back on the ship.'

'They must have done, they were on the late afternoon sailing.'

'No, they did not.'

'Are you absolutely sure?'

'Very sure.' The girl nodded. 'I remember very good, I watch them because she had on such pretty dress and such lovely shoes. They go off that way, and they go in car and drive away. Only then I see the sunglasses. They no get on the ship, I was keeping an eye to try and catch the lady and return sunglasses to her. But the ship leave without them, I am very sure of that.'

'Did they have luggage with them?' Mel asked. What on earth was going on, who were Joshua and Kaylee and why had everyone lied to her? She had trusted them. And she'd trusted Ryan. A sick feeling settled in her stomach. The sky had been forget-me-not blue, but now a large white cloud had come in from the sea and settled over the sun.

'No, no luggage at all.'

'Thank you.'

Mel shivered. Who was Ryan Peacock? she thought, seeing him emerge smiling from the café. Mel instinctively secreted the sunglasses in her handbag. She'd believed she was getting to know Ryan, but suddenly felt duped. In reality, she didn't know him at all. He'd arrived out of the blue, an acquaintance of a short while. A man she had seriously contemplated losing her heart to. Could there be a simple explanation for any of this? Or was she in real danger?

As he approached, the wind whipped up and the second note which had been sitting by her hand flew into the breeze, circling round. She jumped up desperate to catch it but missed as it scudded away along the ground. Ryan ran to get it for her, but now she absolutely didn't want him to see it. She no longer trusted him. She chased after him and the note, watching it turn and tumble crazily towards the quayside where it danced over the cobblestones, tantalisingly out of reach. Then, just as Ryan put his foot down to stop it, the wind whisked it away and down into the harbour waters where on the wash from a boat, it floated, away, away, out of reach.

'Darn it,' he laughed, 'what was that piece of paper all about anyway?' His brows looked arched to her, somehow calculating. Oh heavens, now she was imagining things. She'd always thought he had such a nice face. She didn't know what to think any more.

'It was just a list of things I had to do for Makso, it was nothing, really, I can make a new list.'

Ryan nodded and looked at her curiously.

They sat back down at the table and she said, 'Ryan, I was just wondering. Where's the note with the fingerprints, the one that Joshua tested?'

Ryan looked momentarily lost for words. He searched in his pockets. There was an uncomfortable silence. 'Why, hell, how silly of me, I must have forgotten to get it back from Joshua. I could get him to send it to me when he returns from his cruise.'

'Thank you,' said Mel, but her own voice rang in her ears like a disembodied echo. 'I think we might head home now, I have work to do for Makso and I've neglected it.'

'Is everything ok, Mel? you sound a little tense.'

She collected herself, she wasn't going to be fazed by any of this. If he wasn't who he seemed to be, if Ryan could be a consummate actor, she could be a pretty good actress too. 'Oh,' she laughed it off, 'you'd be tense too if you worked for Makso and had a pile of paperwork waiting for you.'

'I'll give you a lift back.'

'Thank you.' She gave him one of her best smiles. She used it like a mask. She mustn't reveal anything.

They turned the corner and headed for Ryan's car. As if he sensed her unease and wanted to make it better, Mel felt his arm very tentatively land on her shoulder, then his hand crept down and squeezed her arm. All afternoon she'd wanted him to give her some sign he was interested. Now he had, she couldn't wait to shake him off.

With good reason too. For, had she looked back, she would have seen Kaylee and Joshua. Down by the quayside, where they had fished out of the water the second note. As soon as Mel and Ryan were out of sight, they took it to a car in which they drove off, at top speed, in the direction of Pula.

Mihovil liked to keep busy when he was troubled, it was the only way to see off the constant thoughts that invaded his head. He swept the area round the pool with long regular strokes of his broom. He'd been round once already and practically all the needles from the Cedar of Lebanon were neatly swept into the adjacent beds. He was now just going through the motions, thinking, thinking. The needles sat on the red soil like woody confetti helping to keep in the little moisture there was at the height of summer. Decorative red and yellow hibiscus flowers smiled up at him but he couldn't smile back. Austere and sombre woody notes of cedar oil exuded from the branches like the incense at church, as if the tree was trying to soothe Mihovil's agitated soul.

He had noticed through the window into Makso's study, Mel sitting working. She looked troubled too. Usually, she'd come over and say hello but she must have a lot of papers to deal with. There was an uncharacteristic frown on her face and she had been head down in her work ever since she returned from Rovinj. More than once, Mihovil had thought of asking Mel's advice about the deep waters his father had got himself in. She seemed so grounded and understanding. Besides, she was new to the Villa and could see things with a fresh eye. Any advice from her would be wise and practical he was sure. He was about to go over and knock on the French doors for a word when suddenly he heard his name called.

'Mihovil.' He looked around. It was coming from the main gate, and it sounded like Ildie. He dropped his broom and rushed over.

'Come in, come in.' He unfastened it, closing it behind her. She had never been here, but he was rather proud that she should see him in this grand house where he had a proper job and a position of responsibility. Makso and Hiroko wouldn't be back for a while so he made the bold step of inviting Ildie to sit and share some of the homemade lemonade his mother always kept in the pool fridge. 'Come sit in the shade of the trees. How are you? This is such a wonderful surprise.' He was aware of the ice in his glass clinking as his hand shook nervously and he struggled to stop it. He was also crushingly aware of the birth mark on his cheek. As if to cool himself, he put the drink up against it. Pressing the ice cold of the glass to the unsightly mark made him feel that he could dissolve it as he had so often wanted to do. He held the glass hiding the birthmark from her gaze lest his ugliness should offend her.

Amazingly she chose to sit beside him on the bench made for two, not on the chair opposite him as he had thought she would. Her hair was loose today, tumbling over her shoulders like the jasmine tumbling over the wall scenting the garden air. She couldn't have looked prettier with her simple cut-down jeans and white lace top. If only his pulse would stop racing. He longed to look like his trendy cool friends, with their lazy swaggers. But he sat stiff and upright, aware he looked dusty and tousled from all that sweeping.

She didn't seem to notice. 'I have been thinking a lot about what you told me about your father. Neither of us know what it is that he and Makso have become involved in but I always think it is best to be forthright and honest in dealing with people. I have found that out through my own experience.' She looked down, as if she were about to confess a secret. 'Mihovil, do you remember earlier this year? I was terrified when we were queuing to go into the chemistry exam that I would fail. You comforted me, you were very kind. You know I so badly want to be a doctor and my parents are counting on me succeeding. Do you remember I said I felt sick? Mr Tudman took me aside and said I could have five minutes to lie down in the first aid room and pull myself together before the exam started. He is the scariest of teachers, I've always been terrified he will tell me off.

'In fact, the reason I felt ill was because I'd done a very bad thing. I'm ashamed now to tell you about it and I will never do anything like it again. I'd written some chemical formulas on my wrist in biro, and I'd worn a long-sleeved cardigan to the exam. I was going to cheat. Just as Mr Tudman was about to close the door of the first aid room, I told him everything, it just poured out. I thought he would explode and expel me. But, he was so different from his usual way of being. He said I had been silly but by being brave enough to tell him, had given myself another chance. He told me to go to the sink and wash the writing off. He was so nice, I couldn't believe it. He said I was a model student and that I had learned everything I needed to. That I should have confidence in myself, not panic, and I would do well. Do you remember, I went in and I passed with top marks?'

'Yes I do,' Mihovil smiled. He had always thought Ildie was perfect and now he knew she was because she could face up to her mistakes and make things come right. As well as being the most beautiful, divine, elf-like creature he had ever beheld. She was sitting very close to him, so close their thighs were touching.

'What I am trying to say to you is that secrets cause us troubles. Also that sometimes people who are powerful have a front that they put on but that underneath they can be understanding. I think you should be brave and face up to Makso and ask him to help your father. I think you should go to Makso and have it out with him. Tell him that your father is in agony because he cannot repay the loan that paid for your education. Tell him that you are determined to complete your studies, you are an A student, and as soon as you are earning you will pay Makso back, every kuna and more. If only he will let your father off now and never tell your father what you have done. Makso is a man of business. He understands deals. Surely he will be happier to have a loan out to a young man who is going places and will have an excellent career, rather than your father who by his own admission cannot repay the money. This way, your father will save face, you will get your education. Makso will get his money and everyone will be happy. I am sure by being honest and open that is the best way. I know you can sort it.'

'You do?'

'Yes, you can do it. If you want to be a lawyer you will have to face up to difficult and powerful people. You are brave Mihovil. You stood up to that horrible boy who stole my bike last winter. It was you who went to his house and demanded he give it up.'

'But that was easy, Goran saw him take it. I was on solid ground.'

'No, nothing like that is easy but you have courage and kindness and intelligence and ... ' In the silence, she put her hand up to where he was holding the glass against the birthmark, and gently moved it away so his face was revealed. ' ... you are very good-looking when you don't hide your face and ... I love you.'

The world suddenly became an extraordinary place, a bird sang high in the trees and Mihovil half wondered if he had imagined what she had said. But no, he hadn't. For now she was leaning up to him, and he found himself leaning down, and amazingly she placed her hand on his cheek, right on the ugly place and she seemed not to care a jot. And she raised her lips to his and she was kissing him and he was kissing her back and all of a sudden he seemed to have entered another universe, he was in outer space, he was flying. She was flying with him, they were whirling together in that all- encompassing, wonderful, beautiful, life-affirming kiss.

In a moment it was done, in a moment he opened his eyes and she opened hers and they were back on planet Earth. But it was a different Earth to the one he had known because now he was loved by a gorgeous, clever, desirable, girl. Now he was a giant, now he could do anything, anything he wanted. 'I love you too Ildie. You are right, I will face up to Makso, I will help my father out like he has helped me.'

It felt good saying it now, thought Mihovil, with his arm around Ildie's soft shoulders. Anything was possible. But, what he would feel like, standing in front of Makso's tall imposing figure with his eagle eyes boring into him, Mihovil wasn't so sure. All he knew now was that at this moment, he was invincible, totally and utterly.

As he held her, all Mihovil's troubles seemed to melt away. He had been so engrossed in Ildie, he'd barely heard the noise of a car pull up. But now, he could see through the crack at the side of the big gates it was a police car. What's more, one of the policemen had got out and was silently taking photographs of the Villa Lavanda, his camera pointing upstairs, towards the bedrooms. Mihovil squeezed Ildie tighter. He didn't want her to see, didn't want the moment between them spoilt. Then the policeman got in the car and it slowly and silently rolled away. Mihovil was left, his head buried in Ildie's hair trying with all his might to pretend the rest of the world with all its troubles didn't exist. What could all this mean? The worst surely wasn't going to happen. Were the police going to come back, next time to take away his poor father?

6

Mel, sitting in Makso's study, had tried to concentrate on her paperwork and finished half of it. But she was constantly distracted and found herself watching Mihovil sweeping up pine needles. When she next looked, he was chatting to a pretty young visitor, someone Mel had never seen before. Everything was distracting her, her head was full of worries about Ryan and his friends Kaylee and Joshua.

At first when she'd learnt the two Americans had lied and were not continuing on the cruise ship, she was sure Ryan must also know that. But as Mel pondered more and more, it occurred to her that they might have been lying to *him* as well. Maybe she was wrong to suspect Ryan.

Despondently Mel gave up on work, put away her papers and wandered out to the pool area. Makso would be back soon, and she'd rather not have to chat to him about work this late in the day. She'd done what was necessary, ordering some new equipment he'd asked her to, and filed a stack of invoices.

Mihovil and his young friend had gone to sit under the trees where Mel couldn't see them. Then he and the girl emerged and wandered hand in hand towards the gate. Mel held back, not wanting to embarrass him. When he returned to the pool to put away his broom, Mihovil looked flushed.

'Hello Mel, how are you?'

'Fine thank you. What a pretty girl, is she your girlfriend?'

Mihovil walked taller now, his chest puffed out like a proud swan. 'Yes,' he said, nodding his head as if coming to a conclusion, 'yes I would now call her that. She is my girlfriend.'

Mel was pleased, he was such a nice lad. It was good to see him coming out of himself and not being so painfully shy. Was that why Severina had sent the first note asking for help, had she been troubled about Mihovil? Teenagers could be a constant worry. But no, that didn't explain the second note, it was what was going on at the trulli houses that was worrying Severina, and it was something so dire, she needed to keep it a secret.

Suddenly, Mel had an idea. 'Mihovil, I was wondering, you mentioned a while ago that your grandfather keeps a boat in Fazana, do you think he might take me out one day? Maybe this Wednesday evening, perhaps at dusk. I would so love to catch the sunset looking from the sea with my camera.'

'Yes, I can certainly ask him. He would be honoured to show you I'm sure. I can check if he is free Wednesday, but why then? If he can't do then, would you want to go another time?'

'Oh no, Wednesday is best if you could persuade him. It's just that I have a friend coming, an Italian called Cesare. I wanted to show him Makso's yacht, and the Villa Lavanda from that lovely cove. I suppose I want to show off a bit.' Mel was amazed and slightly scared at herself for being able to make up stories on the spot like that. By Wednesday, Cesare would have arrived with Caroline and Antonio for their visit. They were mainly coming to choose Caroline's wedding dress. But it occurred to Mel that this was the perfect plan. She would tell Cesare whom she trusted one hundred percent, all about the second note. They could then go out with Mihovil's grandfather and look at the trulli houses from the safety of the sea. Whatever was going on there would be revealed and Cesare would know exactly what to do.

As she thought about Cesare, Mel pushed to the back of her consciousness the fact that he would be asking her straight out why she had turned down his marriage proposal. She had never talked to a man about her inability to have children but she owed it to Cesare to be straight with him. That would be a difficult conversation so she tried not to think of it. Besides, she was missing him so badly.

'Of course I will ask Grandpapa,' said

Mihovil, clearing away the broom. Then he hesitated. 'There is something I want to ask you, Mel.'

'Fire away.'

'Fire away?' He looked confused.

'It's just an English expression, it means go for it.'

'Ah. I must remember it. The thing is, I need to ask Makso for a favour, and I do not know the best time. My girlfriend,' he smiled as he said the word, like he couldn't hold in his joy, 'she thinks I should ask as soon as he gets back today, but do you think it would be best to wait till tomorrow morning? He has strange moods and I'm not sure which would be best. It is a very important favour.'

As he spoke, they suddenly heard a voice bark out loudly, 'Mihovil.'

It was Makso finally returned with Hiroko from his visit, and he didn't sound happy.

'Yes.' A ll Mihovil's confidence dissolved, and he seemed to shrink as Makso strode up to stand over him.

'Who was that girl I saw leaving my

Villa? Is she something to do with you?'

'Yes.'

Makso's wife Hiroko looked on nervously, her eyes full of compassion for the boy.

'Who said you could invite a complete stranger into my grounds?'

'I am sorry, I didn't think–.'

'No, you didn't, did you?'

'I – '

'Don't answer me back. This is a very busy time for me, I don't want anybody hanging around any of my land who doesn't belong here. Is that clear?'

'Yes.'

'Under any circumstances, do you understand?'

'Perfectly.'

'You have finished sweeping, it must be nearly time for you to go to bed. Get back home.'

With that, Makso marched off, grabbing Hiroko by the hand.

The birthmark on Mihovil's face glowed red, Mihovil put his hand to hide it.

'Are you ok?' Mel was horrified at the humiliation Makso had brought down on the lad, treating him like he was still a child, and in front of other people.

'Yes,' Mihovil bit his lip and worried at the birthmark as if he could rub it away.

'What is wrong with Makso?' She asked. 'He is always scary but usually keeps his temper under control. The other day there was that argument with your father, now this. He is so tense, he is like a bomb waiting to explode.'

'I don't know.' But Mihovil looked troubled.

Mel wondered whether Makso's short fuse was due to whatever was going to happen on Wednesday. After all, there was nothing else wrong that she knew of. The recent art sale had gone well, and Makso's business was thriving. She remembered that only yesterday, he had shouted at Greg Bodie, the groundsman for allowing some contractors clearing trees to take a wrong turn and end up near the trulli houses.

'I must go home now.' Mihovil's brow

was furrowed. 'This is clearly no time to ask the great Makso any favours.'

As Mel watched him leave, she could feel the tension crackle in the air. 'Get here soon, Cesare,' she said under her breath. She couldn't wait for Tuesday to come, the day after tomorrow was when Cesare was arriving in Vodnjan with Caro and Antonio. Then, and only then, would Mel feel safe and among true friends.

Cesare couldn't wait to see Mel. At the airport, he, Antonio and Caroline had hired a car. It was only a short drive to Vodnjan in the hills. Unfortunately Mel was working the evening of their arrival so all they'd managed to do was speak on the phone. But early on Wednesday, they had all arranged to meet up in Vodnjan to drive off to a dress designers in Pula. Then, for later that day, Cesare was delighted to find that Mel had arranged a boat trip for the two of them, just him and Mel, to see the sunset she'd said. It had warmed his heart to be asked, it was the sort of romantic thing two lovers might do. Was she wanting to rekindle their relationship, try again maybe? He hardly dared to hope.

Choosing wedding dresses wasn't really Cesare's thing. Nevertheless, he had volunteered to act as chauffeur and accompany the girls. He welcomed any opportunity to spend time with Mel. He would give his opinion as the token male though he knew nothing about dresses.

Antonio had left for a business meeting with a supplier of Croatian wines who was hoping to strike a deal to supply his hotel, the Girasole. Besides it would be unlucky if Antonio, as Caroline's groom, saw the dress beforehand.

When Cesare saw Mel in the morning, standing waiting for them in the square at Vodnjan, she was even more beautiful than the last time. In a grey cotton dress with a peach-coloured cardi across her arm, she looked fragile. He suddenly became concerned about her. Her collar bone was too prominent, and she had lost a little weight which he didn't agree with. He had been brought up believing women should be woman-shaped. What Mel needed clearly was more of his homemade pasta. But her skin glowed with the kiss of the Croatian sun and her eyes lit up when she saw him. She was a picture standing there in the old medieval square of Vodnjan where for centuries lovers had met and embraced, parted and wept. All human life was here and Cesare didn't know how things stood for them both. Cesare was so nervous, he wasn't sure whether she wanted him to be forward or reserved and he was scared of doing anything to frighten her off.

His dearest wish was to gather her to him and feel her body melt into his. Instead though, he took her hand very formally and kissed it in the old Italian way, with a slight bow. As soon as he'd done it he felt foolish, they had been so close back in Sorrento, now they felt like strangers. He watched as she was swept up by Caroline in a full embrace. He wished he'd been courageous enough to do the same. Nevertheless he thanked the lord he was now in her presence and delighted in hearing the two girls twittering like birds in the back of the car as he drove them.

'Each day I get a different idea about what design would be best,' said Caroline. 'That's why I need you, dear Mel, to keep me on track and help me make a decision. What do you think about something off the shoulder like this?' Caroline showed Mel some photos torn from magazines as they sped off down the road.

'Personally, I think something a bit more elegant with some more detail would be lovely, everyone seems to have off the shoulder these days.'

'I was hoping you'd say that.' Caroline clapped her hands. 'My mother seems set on off the shoulder but I'd like to do something different. What do you think of this one from the designer in Pula? It's very original but I'd have to be really brave and I'm not sure I could carry it off.'

Cesare smiled as he negotiated the streets of Pula. He'd never imagined there'd be so much to say about beads and buttons, silk and taffeta, underskirts and bows.

The designer looked delighted to see them and showed them to a comfortable room all cream carpets, silk curtains and bowls of lilies, with a small round stage in the centre. 'Please sit down, sir. You are the brother of the bride maybe?'

'Just a good friend,' said Cesare as the girls were ushered over to a long rail full of ivory, brilliant white and cream meringue confections. Cesare was brought coffee which was just what he needed and the trying on began in earnest. It was a whirl of satin shoes and jewelled tiaras, veils and pearls and sequins. The girls were in their element. Snatches of the designer's enthusiastic descriptions came to him as he let it all wash joyfully over him. ' … tulle ball-gown skirt … mermaid tail … Sabrina neckline … Venice lace … '

It was a different world. Far from police work, a charming, sweeter world.

Caroline tried on dress after dress, veils and trains were fussed over, sleeves admired, layers of petticoat smoothed down and arranged. Measurements of waists were taken, hair designs and complexions discussed, earrings were tried on and fine silver chains sparkled on flawless skin as a whole ensemble was put together for both the bride and for Mel as the bridesmaid. Finally, the winning styles were chosen.

'Now, one last thing,' said the designer to Mel. 'Come with me, beautiful bridesmaid,' and he ushered Mel and Caroline back into the dressing room. Unsuspecting, Cesare sat wondering if the designer was going to try and change Caroline's mind, persuade her to purchase a more expensive dress. He hoped not, he had liked the dress she had chosen for herself and the dazzling lemon-yellow one for Mel.

Then suddenly, as the curtain moved aside, there was Mel, and she seemed to glow. Cesare was so astounded by what he saw, he stood up and felt himself take a sharp intake of breath. 'Caramia.' The word came involuntarily from his lips. There stood the woman he loved, the woman who had filled his head with thoughts of marrying since the day he met her, the woman who had stolen his heart completely and utterly ... dressed as a bride. She looked ravishing, her dark hair had been swept up in wings either side of her face, and fastened artlessly with pearl clips. Tiny tendril curls dripped down to nestle against her ears.

The dress was perfect for her. Capped sleeves of gossamer lace, lighter than mist, studded with pearls sat like a layer of morning dew across her shoulders. The designer's voice skimmed over Cesare's consciousness saying, 'This dress is of the most perfect Croatian lace. It will become an heirloom, to be passed to future generations. The sweetheart neckline is of brilliant white lace still made by our craftswomen in the traditional motifs of leaves and flowers. See how beautifully it hugs the lady's figure and then dips down to a skirt of such timeless magnificence, falling gently over the hips and demurely to the floor in a delicate train. She looks like she is floating on air, does she not?'

She did, she was the most gorgeous woman in the entire world. Cesare was mesmerised. He felt a tug at his heart so palpable it almost jolted him from where he was standing, and as Mel turned full circle, glittering under the lights he knew there and then she was the only woman he could love.

'I always feel,' the designer droned on, 'that the bridesmaid should be given a chance to think of her own magical wedding one day, as well as the bride.' But Cesare heard nothing, felt nothing but the way he was drawn to Mel, as if two ends of a silken ribbon had been passed round his waist and hers, and was being drawn together. He felt himself step towards her, he found himself standing next to her, she looked up at him and smiled, for one brief moment he imagined her standing by his side at the altar. Then she stepped away, gave him a look of such profound sadness and looked down. It felt like a rejection and he was lost. He reached out to touch her hand but she had turned from him and gone back into the dressing room. The vision had been replaced by reality.

Cesare gritted his teeth. Tonight they were going on the boat trip Mel had arranged. Tonight he would ask her straight out why she had rejected him. What's more, in a moment of impulse he beckoned to the designer and thrust a bundle of notes into his hand. 'I will take that dress, but it is a secret. I want it delivered to my address in Italy please, and whatever you do, do not tell the ladies.'

Back at the Villa Lavanda Greg Brodie was keyed up that Wednesday had at last arrived. He was doing his best to play the part of dutiful groundsman. His nerves were stretched as taut as a string on a guitar. You'd never have known to look at him, fixing the lawnmower on the cool green grass next to the Villa, his tools laid out in precision order. This was the perfect place to be, he could hear what was going on in the kitchen with Severina and Ivan. He was well placed to see Makso and Hiroko's bedroom and could observe the front gate to see who was coming and going.

Mel was out of the way having gone to Pula with those friends of hers and that was a good thing. She was far too inquisitive and far too intelligent for his liking. She wasn't the sort of girl to be inactive, so to have her out of sight gave him some relief in his difficult task.

Nothing but nothing must go wrong. Their big chance was coming, the moment he and his accomplices had been waiting for literally for months. The day he'd worked towards with quiet precision, keeping in the background, making himself useful, recording things mentally and feeding them back. Now the time was nearly here, he could feel his heart pound with tension. The only thing was, unlike Makso with his Croatian hot-headedness, Greg couldn't wear his heart on his sleeve. Couldn't show how keyed up he was. Makso's temper had been rising like a gathering storm for days now. He'd picked fights with everyone. Part of Greg's job was to keep everything as low key as possible, not rock the boat. Greg must keep an eye on all the players and make sure everything went according to plan.

Greg's time in the marines stood him in good stead. There, he'd been trained to observe everything and everyone. He'd been an expert psychologist, taking a keen interest in his men and ensuring the weaker ones were supported, but that they were taken out of the line of action if they couldn't cope. Greg was the one who watched, and listened, learned and acted. He was the one who was always cool whatever the heat. He smiled a wry smile as he tinkered with the lawnmower and watched his own sweat drip liberally onto the machine. The heat of the day mirrored the heat of this whole operation. But he would keep cool inside, his nerves were pure iron. He remembered the motto of the marines and it comforted him, 'per mare, per terram,' by sea, by land. He had kept everything on land ticking over and the operation this evening was moving to the sea, his spiritual home. If he had his way, and he usually did, nothing would go wrong.

He had observed Mel constantly, he knew her movements like he knew everyone else's at the Villa Lavanda. You had to make sure there were no weak links in the chain. As he tinkered and oiled, undid screws and tightened them, he heard Makso come down the stairs and grab his keys. 'I'm out now,' he barked in Greg's direction. 'Make sure you trim those laurels, they're looking scruffy.'

'Will do,' Greg answered, always the faithful servant, always head down doing his work. Always playing the part.

He heard Makso's car roar into the distance. All was quiet, thank heaven. Until Greg heard another car approach. That would be Mel returning from Pula. He heard her say goodbye to her friends, her voice drifting to him on the lavender-scented air: 'See you down at the harbour in Fazana Cesare.'

'Looking forward to it,' came the reply, a deep Italian voice.

It was good she was going out later

with that Italian. They must be going for dinner in Fazana. That was ideal, it would keep her right out of the picture and out of danger on this most important of nights. He heard the car drive off, and Mel's key in the front door, closing behind her. Then Greg's ears picked up another car. They weren't expecting any deliveries or visitors. He was hoping for a quiet afternoon to get his thoughts together. To plan. But it wasn't to be. The doorbell rang, an insistent, impatient chiming.

'I'll go,' he yelled, jumping up, not wanting Mel to answer it. If he was going to keep a lid on things today, he had to control them.

But Mel hadn't heard him, and by the time he got into the hall, she'd already let in two uniformed policemen. That was the last thing Greg needed even though he had a strong suspicion why they were here. He must get rid of them, he didn't want them sniffing round. 'Good afternoon, officers. What do you want?' asked Greg sharply.

'We want to talk to Mrs Yurcich.'

'What for?' asked Mel.

'Is she here?' the policeman persisted, glaring at them both.

'She's–.' Mel began, but Greg stopped her. She mustn't betray that Hiroko was upstairs.

'Not here,' he finished the sentence.

Mel stayed cool, he'd give her credit for that. She'd picked up immediately on his unease though from the frown on her face, she was obviously confused that he'd lied.

'Where is she?' asked the policeman.

'She's gone out.'

'Where?'

'With her husband.'

Mel's eyes bore into Greg. Mel would have seen Makso leave in his posh car, speeding away on his own. She knew Hiroko was upstairs with baby Ivo. Everything about the glance she shot Greg said, 'What are you talking about, why are you lying?'

Suddenly, from upstairs came the sound of the baby crying.

'Isn't that Mrs Yurcich's baby?' asked

the policeman, stepping further into the hallway. There was a movement upstairs. Greg knew he must stay calm.

'Yes.'

'Then Mrs Yurcich is likely to be with him, isn't she?' So saying, the two policemen brushed past Greg and took the stairs two at a time.

Mel, looking alarmed, pursued them. 'Excuse me, what authority do you officers have for going up there?'

Greg sped up. This was one occasion he didn't mind Mel's assertiveness. She always had protected Hiroko and even uniformed men weren't going to stop her. Greg just hoped that Makso's wife had managed to make herself scarce. They arrived in the bedroom, and there was baby Ivo, crying his head off, alone.

'Who is looking after this child?' asked the policeman, suspicion clear in his piercing gaze.

'Miss Sanderson,' said Greg, looking at Mel and willing her with all his might to give the right answer. 'Aren't you Mel?'

There was an uncomfortable silence

which Mel filled by picking up the red-eyed baby and calming him in her arms. Greg held his breath, waiting for Mel's answer, his fists balled at his side, while the policemen turned with their backs to the window and stared him out. Mel stood next to him, facing the balcony. She looked from him to the policemen and back again.

She hesitated, obviously torn between telling a lie to the police and protecting Hiroko. Finally, after what seemed like a lifetime, Greg heard her say, 'Yes, of course I am.' Relief spread through his veins like a tot of whisky. But then, his anxiety rose again like mercury in a thermometer for there, outside the window, across from the pool, he spotted the small dark shape of Hiroko hidden behind the laurel bushes, watching everything going on. He turned to look at Mel and by the slight raising of her eyebrow, he realised she too had caught a glimpse of Makso's wife, hiding. Greg bit his lip. Hiroko mustn't reveal herself, none of this must escalate. Any hint of the police being around would freak Makso out and might jeopardise the operation this evening.

Uncharacteristically, Greg was frozen. He needed to get the police out and away well before Makso's return. He knew too he'd have to try and explain some of what this was all about to Mel once the police were gone, he was sure of that. She wasn't the sort to be kept in the dark for long and yet the more people who knew what was going on the more risky it was. It would be dangerous for her to know too much. His was a tricky balancing act.

The baby started to cry again. 'He's terribly hot,' said Mel to the policemen, 'and you've frightened him storming upstairs like that. I'm going to take him outside in the fresh air.' Without so much as a by your leave, she marched past the policemen and down the stairs. Greg had to admire her pluck. They weren't out of the woods yet though. What if the police decided to search the grounds, what if they scared Hiroko out of her hiding place? That would be a disaster. The poor woman lived in a state of anxiety as it was and people did unwise things when totally stressed, he'd seen it enough times on the battlefield.

The sound of the baby crying at the top of his voice grated on them all. The two policemen went down and stood in the hall, their faces creased with the noise, as a message came through on their radio which they struggled to hear. Greg saw Mel making much of the baby, taking him into the kitchen, near the back door. In the seconds the policemen were preoccupied, Greg glanced into the garden and saw Hiroko had disappeared. She was under such strain, he feared for her. He went to Mel. 'Go and find Hiroko,' he whispered, 'she'll be terrified for the baby.'

'What on earth is going on?' she hissed.

'I'll tell you, I promise, but not now. Please, please, find Hiroko, take the baby to her.'

Mel flared her nostrils at him, she was a force to be reckoned with, but she headed out to the pool area, calming the screaming baby, all the while looking round for Hiroko while Greg went back inside.

'We have an emergency call we must go to.' The policeman resignedly hooked his radio back onto his jacket. 'But we will be back. Tell Mr and Mrs Yurcich we were here today and that we need to speak to Mrs Yurcich. Get her to phone the station immediately she returns.'

'Of course,' said Greg, all polite compliance, his pulse ticking fast at his temple.

With that they were gone. He watched until the police car was safely off in a cloud of dry Croatian dust, then he slammed the door and ran out into the garden.

Neither Mel nor Hiroko were anywhere to be seen. Greg called, 'Mel, Mel.' Then, 'Hiroko, Mrs Yurcich.' Whatever happened he must find them and calm the situation down before Makso returned. Makso must never know the police had been sniffing around.

He hoped to goodness Hiroko hadn't

run out on the road somewhere she would be seen. He shot out and looked hastily up and down. Thankfully, all was quiet. She must have gone out of the garden and into the fields. The worst thing would be if Hiroko went down towards the cove, and worse still if she had led Mel down there, that really would jeopardise things totally. Everything down there would be highly charged getting ready for this evening. It would be a secret hive of activity, things being packed, boats being loaded in the cave so no one would see.

He set off down one of the dust paths, the one Mel had cycled on the day she had encountered the snake and had almost stumbled upon what was going on. There, caught in one of the bushes, Greg saw a blue knitted bootee. He picked it up and stuffed it in his pocket. For once he wished the baby was crying, but if Mel was walking, looking for Hiroko with the baby in her arms, the motion was probably soothing him. Greg ran as fast as he could, stumbling and catching his foot on a stone but he kept on determined not to be thwarted at this late stage.

Finally, he saw the two women. Thank heaven Mel had caught up with Hiroko. The two of them sat in the dust under a tree, Hiroko weeping inconsolably, hugging baby Ivo to her, rocking him back and forth.

Greg ran to join them. Once he had finished panting, he managed to blurt out, 'Is she ok?'

'Yes, I think so,' said Mel, 'now she has Ivo back. What the hell's going on here, Greg? I lied in front of those policemen, I perjured myself and it's all your fault. I can't understand what Hiroko's saying, she's too distressed, she won't speak in English. What on earth was all that about? I only helped to shield Hiroko because I can't imagine for a minute she's done anything wrong. Look at her, she's terrified. This is all really weird, is Makso mixed up in something dodgy?'

Greg knelt down and put his hand on Hiroko's. 'You'd better tell her Mrs Yurcich.' Then his tone became softer.

'Hiroko. She's defended you, she has a right to know. Neither of us want to see you hurt.'

Hiroko's sobbing died down. Ivo was slumbering in her arms, his little face peaceful after all the activity. She clutched his tiny foot where his bootee had fallen off.

Hiroko finally spoke. 'Tell her what?'

But Greg shook his head and said, 'Come on, Hiroko, there's no point pretending in front of me any more, I know your secret.'

'How can you?' Hiroko looked hunted, vanquished.

'I've spent a lot of time overseas. I knew you weren't Japanese from the beginning, I knew you were Vietnamese. You nearly got caught out, didn't you, at Makso's party. Someone told me you couldn't converse with that Japanese businessman. You've been an illegal alien from the time you first set foot in Croatia, haven't you? That's why the police want to interview you.'

'It's true, I have tried to dupe you all.'

A tear squeezed out of her eye and rolled down her cheek. Hiroko bowed her head in shame. 'What are you going to do? I couldn't bear to be without my baby, whatever happens, don't part me from him, he means everything to me.'

She grasped Greg's hand and held it tight. 'Please, please be kind, for the sake of the baby. What are you going to do, are you going to turn me in?'

7

'Turn you in?'

Greg held out his hand and helped Hiroko up. 'Come on, this is no place to talk things over, come back to the house.' Mel supported Hiroko who held the baby, as the three of them walked in silence, each thinking their own separate thoughts. As they stepped into the Villa, Hiroko sat down exhausted on one of the plush sofas, motionless, as if paralysed with fear. Baby Ivo slept in her arms.

'Have you made a decision?' she finally asked, staring at Greg Bodie.

He seemed to be weighing things up in his mind. Then, his chin determined he said, 'And leave little Ivo here in the care of that nurse and Makso? What good would that do the poor little mite?'

For a second, Mel detected not just dislike of Makso in Greg's tone but something bordering on hatred. What had Makso done to generate such high emotions from a practical straightforward guy like Greg? she wondered.

Hiroko's body visibly untensed, the lines on her forehead smoothing. She rocked Ivo and held back tears of gratitude. 'Thank you, thank you so much. I am such a bad woman, I know it, Makso he tells me so.'

Mel felt anger rise in her belly. She put her arm round Hiroko's painfully skinny shoulders to comfort her. 'That's nonsense. From what I've seen, Hiroko, you don't have a bad bone in your body. Surely you and Makso are married, I've seen the photos of the two of you in Vodnjan Church with your beautiful white dress and veil. I really can't see why you would be an illegal alien.'

Hiroko turned her face downwards, too ashamed to look them in the eye. 'Ah I was so happy that day, before things turned bad. Makso, he tells me I am illegal, just two months after that wonderful ceremony in church. I was wanting to go into Pula, I had learned there was a club, a small gathering of Vietnamese women like me, far from home. I had just learned I was pregnant and I was missing my mother and family so badly. I was happy to have found out about this group on the internet. They seemed good people, not just sitting around drinking tea, instead they have a mission. They help many of the poor women who are trafficked from my country into Europe. Women who are tricked by horrible men who promise them jobs and work but then use them very badly, very shamefully. I am now a wealthy woman, married to a rich man and I wanted to help those poor young girls too. Back in my own country I had a job, I looked after elderly people, it was good work. To help those girls in this strange country would have taken my mind off my loneliness here. I thought Makso would be pleased for me to have an interest. Instead he got angry and shouted. He said I was ungrateful and I should have enough here to keep me happy in this beautiful house with him. That's when he lost his temper and told me we are not legally married. He said we only had a church ceremony, not a civil ceremony. There were so many people when we got married, and all speaking Croatian. How was I to know? I would never have broken the law willingly, I have been a stupid and bad woman.'

Mel made a pot of tea and managed to get Hiroko to eat a toasted bun. Then the two women put Ivo in his cradle and Hiroko sank into bed to sleep. When Mel came down, Greg was sitting at the kitchen table deep in thought. 'There's something very odd going on here,' said Mel. 'Why on earth would Makso not go through the proper motions to marry Hiroko legally? It doesn't make sense.' Greg cast her a glance she found difficult to read, but wasn't offering any solutions. 'I have a friend, my previous employer Oscar, he's a very good lawyer. I'm going to ask him to look into things and see if he can help Hiroko.'

'Don't do that,' said Greg, his voice was hard, like a door slamming. 'Don't get involved.' It made Mel jump. But her sense of injustice had been aroused. Just because Greg couldn't be bothered or was too protective of his own job, didn't mean she couldn't help Hiroko. Without saying any more, Mel went upstairs with a determined step to get ready for her meeting with Cesare Mazzotta. She wasn't afraid of Makso although she was beginning to wonder if she was the only person in this house who wasn't.

Fazana was blessed with a white pebble beach which glowed in the late afternoon light as Cesare drove the hire car round to the picturesque harbour. Small but grand houses had been turned into restaurants. Mel was glad to be away from the Villa, she had so much on her mind. She would tell Cesare later what had happened that afternoon with Hiroko. For now, she was pleased of some light relief although she was only too aware that there was a burning question hanging uncomfortably between them of why she had turned down Cesare's marriage proposal. So, she focussed on the mundane and tried to enjoy the beautiful scene.

'The buildings here are painted so prettily,' said Mel. 'That one reminds me of Wedgwood blue porcelain with swags and tails picked out in cream over the windows.' It occurred to her that since she had left her parents at eighteen to study in London, she'd never had a home of her own. After all the dramas of the afternoon, she longed for a sanctuary, a place of peace and tranquillity. As a nanny she'd always lived in other people's houses, always been tangled up in other people's difficulties. She wondered now if she'd ever have her own home.

She watched a lady from one of the houses in the narrow streets by the harbour, absorbed in watering a window sill herb garden and picking off seedheads. Then Mel watched her stand back with a satisfied smile on her face as she greeted her husband emerging from the house. She crushed the herbs in her hand and held them out to him to enjoy the scent. He kissed her cheek before they headed back in to make a home cooked supper. 'They look happy,' said Cesare but there was a sad tone to his voice. Mel stared out of the window. She knew he would soon press her for answers on why she had turned down his marriage proposal. She almost felt like turning back when there at the waterfront, waving and gesticulating to them, she saw Mihovil.

They parked the car and made their way over. 'This is my grandpapa, he is very honoured to be taking out my new friends in his boat.' He looked proud as punch as he introduced them. 'He does not, I am afraid, speak a word of English. He understands though that you wish to see the sunset and to take a little tour around the coastline and look at the Villa Lavanda from the sea. I am so sorry I cannot come too, but Makso has ordered me to help my mother clean all the silver at the Villa. He keeps finding work for us to do in the house. It is like we are prisoners he wants to keep indoors all the time.'

The boat was charming with its gay orange awning. The sea lay calm as Mihovil's grandfather undid the ropes and steered away from the little harbour with its distinct clocktower. As they chugged along, the old man nodded to them to sit on the cushioned seats then tactfully withdrew to his place at the front of the boat. Looking away from them out to sea, it was as if he sensed their need to be alone.

'You looked very pretty in that wedding dress, Mel, even more beautiful than you did dressed as a bridesmaid.'

Mel trailed her hand in the cool aquamarine sea. She didn't know what to say. Cesare needed his answers and he wasn't going to beat around the bush. He opened his mouth to speak again, and placed his hand gently under her chin, making her face him. 'I had hoped one day–.'

'I know.' She stopped him, edging away. It was too painful for words knowing how she had disappointed this gorgeous man, and how she was destined to disappoint him further. As if mirroring her dying hopes, the sun which had blazed bright was dropping in the sky. It was such a sublime evening. If only they were truly lovers, but that could never be. She closed her eyes then opened them again and took the courage to look on Cesare's gorgeous tanned face. 'Cesare, there is something I haven't told you about which is very painful for me. So painful, I have never spoken of it to any man. But – .' His eyes were clear, his loving gaze was all the more agonising because she could not return it. He was framed now by a huge semicircular sinking ball of fire. 'But I know that you love children. You're Italian, from a huge family. Looking forward to babies of your own is in your blood. The thing is,' she scrunched the hem of her skirt between tight fingers, 'that's something I could never give you.' He looked puzzled. 'When I was a child, I was very ill. I had leukaemia and there were times when it looked as if I wouldn't make it. I had so many treatments, I lost all my hair.' He reached out and put his hand to her thick dark hair and the gentle gesture nearly dissolved her. 'But I pulled through. Life is a gift and I was given that gift. But only one life, only mine. The doctors told me that as a result of the treatment, I would never give life to another. I can never have children. I couldn't do that to you, Cesare. You'd make such a perfect father.'

'Caramia, is that it?' His voice was soft. The sky suffused his face with peach and coral. 'Was that why you turned me down?'

'Yes.'

'Dearest, sweetest Mel, I will only ask you one question. For only one question really matters. Please take your time, think carefully. Do you love me?'

Mel listened to the water lapping against the boat, and the seagull's calls as they dived for tidbits on the shore. This place was timeless, Cesare's question was timeless. How many men had asked that of how many women over the centuries? Some destined to be overjoyed, some to be crushingly disappointed. She looked at his fine bone structure, his kindest of kind eyes, and realised she didn't need any time to think about her answer. 'Of course I do, I've been in love with you from the first moment I saw you. But it's not to be–.'

He took her hand, he held it tight. 'Then that is ALL that matters. For I know that you are the one I want, and only you. If children came that could have been so wonderful. But what I want, what I really need is your warmth, your beauty, the joy of being with you. That is enough. It doesn't matter one bit if we can't have children. Not one bit. I will understand and I can accept. YOU are all I need. Mel. I love you with all my heart. Let us try one more time. Tell me you will marry me. Please.'

He held her hand and she could feel he was shaking. The truth in his gaze wiped all of her painful worries away. Together maybe they could make it work. Before she knew it, she heard herself say, '... if you're sure.'

His smile was as big and bright and

all-encompassing as the massive sun on the horizon. 'Of course I'm sure. I have never been so sure about anything.'

'Then yes, Cesare. If you are sure it doesn't matter, I will marry you.'

He gathered her in his arms, placed a kiss on the top of her head and the two of them watched the magical sight of the sky melding from orange fire to glowing embers. Mel had truly never felt happier. Maybe she would now have a home to call her own. Like the two people in the harbourside house, she and Cesare, just the two of them alone could be happy.

Mihovil's grandfather glanced back and smiled and nodded his head as the boat continued chugging through the water. They went on for a few minutes in silence. As they rounded the cove, Mel remembered the reason she had brought Cesare here.

'Look, Cesare,' she said, sitting up. 'There in the distance up the hill you can just see the lights of the Villa Lavanda, and below it is the cove where Makso's yacht is moored. Somebody wanted me to come and see it this very evening, I wanted you to see it too. What on earth do you think they are loading on and off that boat there? It's a pity it's nearly dark now. My eyes are good but I can't make out what's going on.'

'These will help.' From out of his jacket pocket, Cesare took a set of binoculars. 'I brought these special night vision binoculars, they even have thermal imaging.'

Mihovil's grandfather had started to take an interest too, and pointed as if to say did they want to go closer to the shore. Cesare shook his head in a brisk, 'no', and motioned to him to cut off the motor to make them less obtrusive. They appeared to be just a fishing boat searching for the first catch of the evening. The boat bobbed and drifted on the gentle swell, quietly and slowly closer to land. 'What can you see?' whispered Mel.

'They are definitely bringing down a fair quantity of goods, all crated up. There are large flat ones being carried by two men and some smaller boxes, all different sizes and shapes. Some are long, some are squat and flat.'

'Where are they bringing them from?'

Cesare tilted the binoculars upwards. 'They seem to be coming from those little trulli houses, it's like there's a whole mini business going on there.'

'One that Makso doesn't want anyone to know about. Are they loading the stuff straight onto the boat?'

'No. They're putting everything very carefully on the floor of that cave as if they're getting it ready to load on the boat in one go. The cave's obviously a storage place, easy to hide. There's only a small entrance, well camouflaged with overhanging bushes but when you focus on it, you can see there's a heavy set of lockable gates. There's another couple of guys who are bringing some sort of supplies off the boat and loading them into the trulli houses. I guess until they load all those things in, they won't have enough room to take the other things out of the cave and into the boat. Here, take a look through these, they're very high tech, with a strong resolution. Tell me if you see anyone you recognise.'

Mel took the binoculars. Their little boat was drifting way to the side of the cave, out of the way. She studied the moving figures. 'Well, I'd say that tall rangy guy pointing and ordering everyone around is definitely Makso. He's right at the centre of everything. I can't say I recognise any of the others.' She scanned around the cave, and on the beach. Then, catching something else on the thermal imager, high above the cave she said, 'Wait, I think there's a dog or something cowering in the bushes above. No, it isn't a dog at all, it's a person lying down, on their own. They've just stood up, it's a man, he looks familiar. I think from the height of him, the glasses and the amount of hair, it's Greg Bodie. What on earth is he doing skulking round there? Do you think he's acting as some sort of look-out?'

'Here, let me see.' Cesare took the binoculars as the figure began to wave. Without the binoculars, the sky was so dark now, Mel could see very little. Then, suddenly, she saw a tiny beam of light flashing on and off at them through the bushes. On, on, on, off, off, off, deliberately. 'What's going on, Cesare? Is that Morse code or something?'

Cesare waited, quietly focussing on the light flashing on and off. Then, moving swiftly, he tucked the binoculars back in his jacket, reached to the side of the boat, grasped one of the emergency oars which sat on hooks inside the boat, and thrust it into her hand. 'What are you doing?'

Both Mel and Mihovil's grandfather stared in amazement. 'We've got to get out of here now,' hissed Cesare. 'And quietly, it's not safe. Paddle quickly but don't splash, don't make a sound.' So saying, he grasped the other oar, pressed his fingers to his lips so that Mihovil's grandfather understood not to start the motor, and started paddling away, retracing their route back towards the harbour.

As soon as they were at a safe distance Mel asked, 'Could you read the signal? What was he saying?'

'No, no I couldn't.'

'Then shouldn't we have stayed to find out more about what was going on or call the police or something?'

'Don't worry, I'm going to call them myself. In the meantime Mel, I want you to do nothing. I want you to act perfectly normally when you go back to the Villa. Please don't do anything untoward, my darling. Don't mention what we saw to anyone and don't challenge Makso or Greg or Severina or anybody else, do you understand me?'

'Yes, perfectly.'

'I'm going to drive you back now, and on the way, you're going to go through everything again, the notes thrown onto your balcony, everything that's happened with Ryan Peacock, and don't leave out a single detail. I'm going to contact my superiors and extend my leave. Believe me, I'm going to get to the bottom of this, and quickly.'

When Cesare got back to his bedroom in Vodnjan he wasted no time in speaking to his boss. 'I am very grateful, sir,' he ended up, 'for you agreeing to give me time to pursue this case covertly. You won't regret it.'

'One thing, Mazzotta.'

'Sir?'

'Don't step on any toes of our Croatian friends. Remember you don't have any jurisdiction there. We can unearth things, and I have heard for some time that there is corruption in the local force, but go carefully. People with money like Makso Yurcich have friends in very high places. You will also have to act quickly. I fear things will be moving very fast now.'

Cesare knew that only too well as he got out his notebook and made detailed notes of everything Mel had told him. If she heeded his warning and didn't set a foot out of place, she could stay safe. The trouble was, he knew her feisty nature. Late though it was, he phoned his young colleague Tomasso back in Sorrento and instructed him to run further checks on those at the Villa Lavanda. It was just as he was putting the phone down that it vibrated in his hand, this time ringing with an unknown number.

'Hello.'

'Commissario Mazzotta?'

'Yes.'

'You don't know me. My name is Greg Bodie. I was signalling to you this evening. I think from the way you withdrew your boat, you understood my message.'

Cesare's eyes narrowed, this could be the breakthrough he needed to keep Mel from danger. His heart beat like a woodpecker on a treetrunk. 'I did.'

'Good. I need to explain things, and I need to set up a meeting with you and a colleague of mine. Can you meet me at the back of the church in Vodnjan, first thing tomorrow?'

It was a bright sunny morning and Mihovil had had a dreadful night's sleep. On waking early, he decided he could wait no longer to approach Makso about his father's debt. His father had been so tense lately. Even Mihovil's grandfather had asked him yesterday when they were waiting by the boat at Fazana harbour, 'What is wrong with your papa? I am so worried about him. One minute he is morose and brooding, the next he is twitchy and jumpy. He will not tell me, his own father, what is wrong.'

Mihovil knew it. He had even heard his mother and father having words through the walls the other night, and they never usually argued. So, this morning he had decided to go to the Villa before breakfast and ask for an audience with Makso.

His heart was pounding as he knocked on the door of Makso's office. Always an early riser, Mihovil knew Makso had been at his desk for hours. Even so, today, his eyes looked even more hooded than normal, not so much tired as haunted.

'What is it you want? I have much on my mind.'

Mihovil had rehearsed this meeting a hundred times. He decided to approach it in the way he had when friends of his had challenged him to dive off cliffs into the sea at Cape Kamenjak to prove his bravery. He had decided then that he wouldn't stand on the brink like many of the other boys, waver, wander a little at the top then teeter on the edge and finally fall off like a leaf. No, he had decided to take a determined ten paces back and then run to the edge of the cliff and launch himself off with a leap like a great soaring cormorant. He tried to conjure up that bravery.

'I have come to speak to you about my father.'

'What about him?'

'I know he is afraid of you, and I know why.'

Makso's mouth moved into a sneer. 'And he has asked you to come here, the brave avenging son to save him from his obligations because he is too feeble to sort out his own problems.'

Mihovil felt his hackles rising to hear his father mocked. 'He hasn't asked me at all, he hasn't breathed a word to me about the debt you placed him under or the secrets you share together.'

'Then if he hasn't told you, who has?' As Makso came round the desk to stand over Mihovil, the boy felt his bravado evaporate. 'It's your mother, isn't it? You and Severina are very close. Has she been plotting against me? Who else has she involved? Like rotten worms in the centre of an apple, you and others are trying to destroy me.'

'No, she's got nothing to do with my coming here today. I haven't spoken a word to her, I only found out by–.'

But Makso raised his hand and wouldn't hear any more. He spoke through gritted teeth. 'Get out of my sight. I can bear your treachery no longer.'

However much Mihovil tried to put his case, Makso wouldn't listen. He was even more dictatorial than usual. Mihovil, deep in despair, left as he had been ordered. What had he done? Surely he hadn't now got his poor mother into trouble? He couldn't bear that.

Mel was full of trepidation coming down to breakfast. She now knew that Makso was up to no good. She'd seen him skulking around under cover of night but she must act normally as Cesare had insisted. Makso was already sitting at the table when she arrived. The dark shadows under his eyes appeared even darker and he kept fiddling with the rings on his fingers as if he was agitated. This was most unlike his usual cool self. 'I have a large amount of documents I signed last night and which I would like you to copy today and get sent off.'

'Of course.' She found it hard to force down her mango and yoghurt this morning, and at every word she felt as if she would choke. As he talked to her, he seemed for some reason to be studying her. Then he said, 'Let me get you some coffee, you look tired.'

She tried to smile and hoped it didn't come out as a grimace while he turned to the sideboard and poured her a large cup. 'Here, drink that up. I have added some of our home-produced honey, you should try it.'

She was grateful for the hot sweet liquid, the caffeine hitting her right in the heart, and she felt a little better as she saw

Makso smile in her direction. 'I am very pleased with all the sales we have made recently, but all the goods need customs certificates and shipping documents. If you have finished your coffee and are ready, I will show you what needs to be done.'

They got up and made their way to the office. Makso installed her by the photocopier with a huge pile of forms marked with post-its. It all looked perfectly in order until she found herself feeling slightly out of sorts. Things had been so busy lately, and so trying. 'Do you think I could have a chair?'

'Of course.'

Makso's steel-grey eyes swam before hers as he observed her intently. 'You have been very busy lately.'

'Yes, but there's nothing I can't cope with.' Her legs felt wooden and heavy, and as she took the weight off them she found she had to hang on to the photocopier to steady herself.

'Oh,' said Makso, 'I don't doubt it. I have kept a very close eye on you and

I have people in this house who are exceedingly loyal to me who have also been interested in your movements. You have been very busy.'

Mel felt a sick feeling in her stomach. Who had been watching her? Had Greg Bodie been tracking her? Her thoughts were becoming fuzzy. She tried to act normally, but as she went to reach her hand out to the papers to start copying them, she became clumsy. Her hand instead of grasping a sheet fell heavily on the pile of papers, knocking everything to the floor. 'I'm sho sorry.' It was as if she was drunk, her head began to swim, her speech to slur. What on earth had been in that coffee?

Makso's voice grated. 'I suppose you think you were very clever. Hiroko's nurse heard you on the phone through the door. It was she who alerted me to the fact that you have a policeman boyfriend. I suppose the two of you thought you would spy on me. You ungrateful woman, I give you a job and let you into my home and that is how you repay me.

It seems my world is full of ungrateful women. Hearing of your treachery, I instructed Hiroko's nurse to tell me of anything she discovered which sounded odd. Imagine my dismay when she told me she saw notes being thrown onto your balcony in secret by Severina. Severina who has always been as loyal as the day is long. Then you come into my house and she forms a vile alliance against me.' Makso's tones clanged in Mel's ears like the church bell at Vodnjan. Nothing felt normal. She put her hand to her forehead, but she was so disoriented that that simple act unbalanced her until she felt herself topple off the chair. By then though, all feeling had escaped her and Mel barely even felt her numb limbs as her body crumpled unconscious onto the carpet at his feet.

When Mel woke, she felt a hard wooden slatted bed beneath her. It took a while for her eyes to adjust, it was so dim with the only light coming in through a small high window. She was in a tiny barely furnished room with just a table under the window and on the other wall, a further bed. The only sounds which came to her were seagulls outside and the rush of the sea against the shore. When her eyes did finally focus, she realised she wasn't alone. There was a figure, motionless on the other bed. She pulled herself together and rose unsteadily on her feet. As she made her way gingerly over to the other bed, she felt her muscles coming to life. As she peered over the motionless figure, she saw sleek black hair and a familiar face. 'Severina?' Mel reached out and shook the figure and was full of relief when she heard Severina moan gently as she came into consciousness. 'Severina, wake up. Where on earth are we?'

Cesare hadn't slept all night and now he was waiting, as instructed, in the front pew of the deserted church in Vodnjan. Greg Bodie had been too security conscious to talk to him over the phone last night, preferring to meet face to face. Cesare heard the huge wooden door bang behind him and turned to see two men enter the church. One, with blond curly hair and a determined gait, led the way. The other, taller, smoother, with a sharp suit and a beard followed. 'Thank you for coming, Commissario Mazzotta.' The curly-haired one looked intently at Cesare through thick-rimmed glasses and shook his hand with a firm hold. 'I'm Sergeant Greg Bodie, formerly with the Met in London and now with the International Crimes task force, and this is my colleague Sergeant Ryan Peacock of the City of New York police. We've been working here undercover for some time but are pleased to have the help of one of our Italian colleagues. That is, if you're willing to come on board to help us defeat Makso Yurcich …'

'Of course,' said Cesare, 'tell me everything.'

Cesare listened intently as the two men told of their comings and goings, of their covert operations and the evidence they had gathered. At the end, Cesare found his shoulders tensed with the effort of taking it all in. It was some operation.

'Surely it's time we told Mel what's happening at the Villa Lavanda, don't you think?' asked Cesare.

'Yup,' said Ryan, 'it is time now. We wondered, for a while, if she were one of Makso's accomplices. It took us a while to check her out but now you're on the scene to vouch for her, it's different. Have you spoken to her this morning?'

'No,' said Cesare, 'not yet. I'll try her now, and get her to come here to meet us. For her own safety, she needs to be out of there.'

He tried the number, then his face fell. 'Her phone is dead. She never switches it off, she always answers when I call, and now there's nothing.'

8

Mel's legs and tummy were still wobbly as she sat on the bed next to Severina, but her head was as clear as the crystal-blue sea crashing on the waves below. 'Severina, you have to wake up. What's going on here?'

Severina's eyes flickered then blinked. 'I feel very strange.'

'You've been drugged.' Mel felt the other woman's forehead and stroked the hair off her brow. Severina was always so neat and tidy, it felt wrong for her to be dishevelled.

'Drugged?' She sat up. 'Makso ... Makso he asked me to try the honey.'

'That was it.' Mel sat beside her. 'For some reason, he wants us both off the scene. I wish I knew what was going on.'

'And the trouble for me,' Severina bit her lip, stemming tears, 'is that I know too much.'

'Too much about what?'

'About the evil Makso is doing. Please, Mel.' Severina grasped Mel's hand as tightly as a drowning woman grabbing a life-raft. 'We have to get out of here and raise the alarm.' She stood up. 'Help me onto this table. I need to see outside.'

'No way,' said Mel who even though she felt decidedly queasy knew the older woman would be more affected by the chemicals in her bloodstream. 'I'll get up there.' The two of them lifted the table to the window and placed it carefully down so as not to make any noise.

'What can you see?' asked Severina.

Mel peered carefully through the small window and whispered, 'We must be locked in one of the trulli houses. I can see the path leading to the cove on the right-hand side, and the track back into the fields in the direction of the Villa Lavanda on the left.'

'Can you see anybody?'

'No, I can hear sounds of someone in the house next door, banging and scraping. It sounds like a workshop. Oh, no wait. There is a man, pacing up and down smoking a cigarette. He's very burly, dressed in black jeans and black t-shirt. Oh, Severina, I think he's here to keep guard on us. Even if I could fit through this window which I don't think I could, he'd be sure to spot me.'

'Come down,' hissed Severina. 'Don't let him see you. What are we going to do?'

Mel climbed back onto the floor and together they silently replaced the table. Mel sat back down beside Severina on the bed and held her hand. 'Look, here's a plan. For the time being, we can't get out of here. But that guy outside doesn't know how long the drugs Makso gave us will work. If we hear a key in the lock we should pull the covers back over ourselves as if we're still out cold. At least that way their guard will be down. If he has an accomplice, or if Makso comes to check things, maybe we'll get to hear what they plan to do with us. There's a saying in English, 'forewarned is forearmed,' it'll give us the upper hand. If we stay passive, they won't expect it when we fight back, and we are going to fight back, believe me. We just have to choose the right moment.'

'All right,' said Severina. Her eyes were brighter now as if she had gained some of Mel's strength.

But even though Mel wasn't showing it, she wasn't feeling totally strong. Her stomach churned, reacting to the sleeping draught. 'In the meantime,' she said, breathing deeply to stem the nausea, 'you must tell me all that you know. What on earth is Makso up to?'

Mihovil had looked everywhere for his mother. This wasn't like her. She always told him if she was going to the shops or popping into Vodnjan. Not only was she not in the kitchen where she normally would be at this time in the day, but she had left the washing-up. The work surface was littered with crumbs, peelings from the fruit she had prepared lay unattended and a fly had settled there. This was so unlike his neat, orderly, organised parent. He set about tidying the dishes, wiping the tops and putting things away. His beloved mother had always told him, 'When you are worried about anything you should do something useful. It'll chase away your fears and get your mind working properly on the problem.' She was so right, so wise. As he briskly clattered and put things right his mind was getting ordered too.

His quick intellect churned over, then a sudden feeling of dread struck Mihovil, constricting his chest. He thought of the odd way Makso had been acting lately, watching Mihovil and his mother. He'd got them to do endless tasks, finding extra work at the Villa as if he feared them going out. Thank goodness Makso was out of the way for once. Baby Ivo had been ill, and he and Hiroko were closeted upstairs with him. Might Mihovil's mother's sudden disappearance have something to do with Makso's increasing shiftiness? Mihovil would have aired his suspicions with Mel but he had already searched for her high and low and she too, oddly, was nowhere to be found.

His mind then switched, like a computer working its way through a programme to some words his grandfather had said after taking Mel and her Italian boyfriend on his boat.

'How was it, Grandpapa, did they have a nice time?'

'Yes my boy, they saw the sunset and held hands, and billing and cooing like rock doves. An old man can tell when a young couple are in love. But then it all changed when we went past the cove near the Villa. The Italian man became very protective, drawing your friend Mel aside as if to shield her. He was watchful like there was something going on there which might harm her.' At the time Mihovil wrote off his grandfather's musings as those of an old man with a romantic imagination. Now the words clanged in his ears like an alarm.

The cove, of course. Why was he fooling around here when his mother and Mel could be in danger? He ran to get his jacket, jumped on his bicycle and started peddling as fast as he could down the dirt track, dust billowing out behind him, through the fields and down towards the sea.

Greg, Cesare and Ryan marched out to Ryan's smart hire car, careful not to run and attract attention. In a sleepy hilltop town like Vodnjan, anything untoward — three sharp-suited men, foreigners obviously on a mission — could have sparked comment which might have got back to Makso. Anything that would alert him could not only scupper the operation which Greg had been working on for so many months, but may well endanger Mel.

Ryan manoeuvred the car out of the street by the church and away from Vodnjan. Cesare, unable to get an answer from Mel's mobile, had phoned the Villa and still got no reply. 'I think,' Greg had said, 'that we should go down to the cove and search those trulli houses openly. Knowing Mel, she may well have gone down to investigate herself. She's not one to sit around doing nothing. Don't worry,

Cesare, she'll be ok. It's probably just that her mobile signal is bad from there.'

His words were unconvincing. Cesare was tense, his hands tightly gripped on his knees. He channelled his detective training. Getting the facts straight would take his mind off the fact that the woman he planned to spend the rest of his life with was in serious danger. 'So let me get this clear,' Cesare turned to Greg, 'Makso has been running not just a fine art business but a skilled operation forging perfect copies of works of art.'

'That's right,' Greg nodded. 'It was Ryan's team in New York that spotted a new player in the market. Cleverly, Makso has chosen not to work at the top end, in the millions. He knows there is heavy scrutiny of very expensive items. Nevertheless the works he has forged have changed hands for tens of thousands of dollars. They're making him very rich. It started when Ryan's team had a call from a New York dealer. His client had bought two Assyrian reliefs of soldiers and horses purportedly from 600bc. The dealer bought them in good faith from a highly reputable auction house. The provenance was all in place, auction catalogues from the 1920s, letters regarding purchases, certificates of authentication. You see, Makso doesn't just have the item itself forged, his forger creates a whole credible story around each one. The client was so proud of his purchase he wanted a friend at the Metropolitan Museum of Art to see them. This friend had a colleague who has studied that period in history all her life. Imagine the dealer's horror when this colleague noticed in the cuneiform inscription, a spelling mistake! It is often simple things like this which trip up a criminal. When the dealer informed Ryan's team, they put out feelers to the Arts and Antiquities Unit of Scotland Yard. It turned out there were suspicions about a few recent sales, all pointing towards Makso Yurcich but nothing yet that could be proven. That's where I came in, as some had turned up in London. When Makso advertised for a handyman, it was an ideal ploy for me to go under cover at the Villa.'

'If it weren't for that mistake, I guess Makso would go on with his shady business for years,' Cesare said.

'Absolutely,' Greg replied. 'Once discovered, this sort of crime can rock the art market to its core. It's been necessary for us to gather as much information as possible to compile a watertight case. I now have copies of documents, mobile phone records, dates of shipments and sales, and intelligence on his next shipment. You and Mel witnessed half of it being loaded last night. That's why I had to signal you to keep away. It hasn't reached its destination yet which we've discovered is Paris. We're tracking it. It will reach the French coast later today, when our colleagues will swoop on it.'

Cesare held on to his seat as the car negotiated twists and turns on the route heading towards the sea. 'You said there were corrupt police here who have turned a blind eye.' Ryan was taking the back roads, which would approach the cove from the opposite direction to the Villa Lavanda.

'That's right. Going undercover at the Villa I have been able to identify materials coming in to the cove which have been sent straight up to the trulli houses. One of the houses contains Makso's master forger. A self-taught artist and near recluse who was running his own highly specialised and small operation. Makso discovered what he was up to. He blackmailed him into the option of being revealed to the authorities and jailed, or moving his wife, children and extended family of aunt and uncle into the trulli houses above the cove. Those poor people know nothing about the illegality of the operation. At night I have managed to sneak down and take photographs. There is a workroom with a small furnace for melting silver, and scattered over the different trulli houses are all that is needed to make a variety of items: silver, rare stone, marble, replica metal and glass. The work of the forger is meticulous, he is obsessive about his art.'

They were close to the cove now, Ryan had turned off the engine and the car was coasting silently at a snail's pace down the unmade dirt track. The trulli houses slumbered in the distance, shimmering under the heat of the day.

'Makso's downfall is that he has become greedy, the slow trickle of items he started with is turning into a torrent. If he had continued to issue the forged items bit by bit we might not have traced them back to him. But, he is like most criminals. He's drunk with his power over people and has begun to think he is invincible.'

'But,' Cesare's hands were balled into fists, 'a man like that will be dangerous when cornered.' He tried Mel's number again. Nothing. 'If he has done anything to hurt Mel . . . '

'Stay cool, my friend,' said Greg and clapped a warning hand on Cesare's arm. 'I've had to stay patient for months. We mustn't blow the operation now.'

Suddenly, Cesare tensed, his alert eyes fixed on a point ahead. 'Mamma mia.

Stop the car. Is that not the boy Mihovil crouching in the grass above the trulli houses? What does he think he's doing?'

Mihovil lay flat as a snake, his gaze fixed on a massive man who paced up and down, his five o'clock shadow and constantly watching eyes making him look like a nightclub bouncer. Why would a man like that be hanging round here? thought Mihovil? Unless he was guarding something. Or somebody. Should he go down and confront the man? Should he telephone the police? To tell them what? That he had vague suspicions and that his mother had been missing all of two hours? They would tell him to run away and stop bothering them. Or worse still contact Makso, who would have him spirited away too. Or maybe take it out on his poor father, who was already entwined in Makso's web of blackmail and lies.

It was as all these questions were whirling like a tornado in his mind, that Mihovil heard a mobile phone ring and watched as the burly man took his out of his pocket. 'No, they haven't made a sound, boss. I will go and look,' the man said. Who hadn't made a sound? Mihovil's hair stood up on the back of his neck, his mouth became dry as a desert. The man swung round and went towards the closest trulli house. Taking a key out of his pocket he put it in the lock and disappeared inside.

Tense minutes passed. Time stood still. All Mihovil's senses were on edge. Suddenly, Mihovil heard a woman's cry. Instinctively he shot up out of the grass, breaking cover. As he did so, he heard footsteps crunch on the path behind him. There was Greg, Cesare Mazotta and another guy hurtling towards him. Mihovil didn't know what to do, who to trust. All he knew was the woman's cry might belong to Mel, or his mother. So he ran, half falling, arms flailing, towards the trulli house.

On hearing the key in the door, Mel and Severina had lain like statues under their covers. Mel's heart had beaten so wildly against her ribs she was sure its thumping would betray her. One eye shielded by her arm, partially open, she sneaked a look at the man. He looked more brawn than brain. He scuffed his feet, looking bored. Having peered at the two women and decided they were still unconscious, he sighed, turned his back on them, took out a cigarette and proceeded to light it. The tension running through Mel was nearly unbearable. The door, their escape route, was wide open. His guard was down. Suddenly, deep in her stomach Mel felt a nausea so acute, she knew her body wanted to rid her of the last of the sleeping draught Makso had administered. If she didn't stretch her cramped body, if she didn't breathe deeply she knew she'd be violently sick and give them away. She he had to do something, this might be their only chance.

On impulse, she shot out of bed and thrust her foot with all the power she could muster into the back of the guard's knee. Screeching, 'aaaieeeee', he toppled like a collapsed easel to the floor. Severina screamed. Suddenly, there appeared Mihovil. In a flash, the boy grabbed the heavy door and whacked it with a sharp crack into the stunned guard's head. Before Mel knew what was happening, men arrived, yelling at the top of their voices in Italian and English. Everything was a crazy blur, then Cesare was at her side. 'Mel, are you ok?'

There was a tangle of arms and legs and shouting. Greg, and Ryan of all people wrestled the guard to the floor. What was Ryan doing here? She was completely confused, but immensely grateful. Mihovil was comforting his mother whose endearments of, 'oh my dear boy, my best boy,' filled the air. Most blissfully of all, the sudden excitement had stopped Mel from being sick. When Cesare gathered her in her arms she had never felt better. Never more secure, never more relieved to see anyone.

Back at the Villa Lavanda, Mel and Severina were left to wait in the car with Mihovil while Greg, Cesare and Ryan swooped on the house. The detectives caught Makso as he ran into the driveway, scrambling to get in his car and make his escape. The game was up and he knew it. Mel's head was now together. All the pieces of the puzzle were falling into place. How both Greg and Ryan had been acting undercover all along, and had played their parts like actors on a stage. How Severina had suspected something and had tried to warn Mel by throwing those notes asking for help. How Mihovil knew his father was under Makso's thumb but didn't know the whole story. How her own beloved Cesare had been sucked into the mystery and had fought to save her.

Mel, Severina and Mihovil were sent in to help comfort Hiroko. She was as stunned as anyone to find out her controlling husband was a criminal. Willingly, she gave a full statement to Cesare. As Mel hugged Hiroko, Severina cradled the baby. Mel was touched how kind and sensitive Cesare was when questioning Makso's wife. What's more, he explained how Makso had lied to Hiroko about the status of her marriage, it had been legal and she could stay in Croatia. 'I have seen bullies like him before. They weave lies like spiders in their horrible webs. Most of us are honest, that is how the world works, but his sort lie to further their own ends. We do not suspect it. So, like butterflies trapped in their webs we find ourselves struggling and then giving up. Do not be defeated, Mrs Yurcich. Think of your little son, he needs you to be strong.'

It all seemed a million miles away now, as Mel gazed in the mirror. There she stood, next to Caroline. They wore wedding dresses, lace and silk confections they had tried on back in the fitting room in Croatia. 'A double wedding with my best friend,' Caroline beamed as she adjusted Mel's veil. 'That's just amazing that Cesare bought your dress in secret and put it away hoping this day would come. Who'd have thought that under that serious exterior there could be such a romantic man?'

Mel couldn't stop smiling. 'He's always

surprising me, and he's nothing if not persistent. He always gets his man.'

'And his woman so it seems.' They both laughed. 'Are we ready to go down do you think?' asked Caroline.

'Yes, as long as I can stop these butterflies whirling around my tummy.' They were at the Girasole, the hotel in Sorrento which Caroline now ran alongside Antonio. 'I can't thank you enough, Caro, for suggesting I be allowed to hijack your wedding day. I wouldn't have wanted to get married anywhere other than in Sorrento where our whole adventure began. Where I met Cesare, and where you met Antonio. I can't believe how much has happened since we came here to do up the beach house. And now here we preparing for a double wedding.'

'It was the boys' idea,' said Caroline. 'They cooked it up together over numerous glasses of Prosecco and I agreed it would be brilliant. You've always been more like a sister to me than anything. And besides, how could I have any nerves when you're here sharing this wonderful day.'

A small whirlwind entered the room in the shape of Izzy, who Mel had cared for over the years as her nanny after Izzy's mother died. Izzy looked like a young lady now. Especially in the beautiful lemon-yellow bridesmaids dress, bought from the Croatian designer and specially altered to fit her slender body. In that wonderful phase between childhood and turning into a woman, Izzy still had her buoyant puppy like enthusiasm for life. She had been rushing back and forth, peering over the banister to check progress downstairs. 'They're all ready for you. Listen, they're playing the wedding march. Oh, don't you look gorgeous, my two most favourite people in the whole world.' Izzy handed each of the brides their bunches of flowers. Waxy gardenias, heady-scented jasmines, sunshine-yellow rosebuds, decorated with tiny wired pearls. She clung to her own bouquet, pretty as a princess.

At that moment, dressed in a sharp

suit, Izzy's father Oscar appeared at the door. For a second, he couldn't catch his breath but just stood there nodding. If Mel wasn't much mistaken, might that be a tear at the corner of this usually totally professional lawyer's eye?

Oscar wandered over and offered his arm to the two women. 'I have never seen my sister looking so radiant,' he beamed at Caroline. 'And Mel, you look superb, Cesare is lucky to have you. I was worried when you left us. It was like losing a member of the family. But here you are, and now I'm going to give you both away, to new lives, with wonderful husbands.'

They set off together, slowly walking in procession down the stairs. A roomful of happy guests turned their faces upwards to greet the bright young people. Mel was overwhelmed. There was Mihovil and his father, for once out of his working clothes all scrubbed up and so proud of his son who was destined for great things. Severina sitting between them glowed as she looked upwards. Even Hiroko, delicate as a reed, dressed in a mint-green dress and summer coat was there, with baby Ivo fast asleep, good as gold.

As they reached the bottom of the stairs, Mel's gaze alighted on Antonio. Looking youthfully elegant, his unruly hair smoothed down for once, he only had eyes for Caroline. Next to him, his dear friend Cesare, handsome as a Roman god, chest puffed up like a peacock to see Mel heading towards him.

The ceremony passed in a whirl of vows, and smiles, blossom and hugs. Once the formalities had been completed, the entire wedding party processed out of the hotel, down the winding road towards the lemon grove. 'Did you know,' asked Cesare as he waved at Hiroko, 'that Hiroko is going to open her very own charity for trafficked women in Croatia? She looks so much stronger.'

'It's turning into a magical day,' said Mel. 'I swear, there are no guests as noisy as Italians. Look at them trying to encourage the Brits to undo their ties and loosen up. Caroline, who put up these bowers of jasmine and lemon blossom over the road? It's gorgeous, like a flowered arch.' Mel could barely make her voice heard above the chatting and laughter.

'Beatrice and Rafaele put up the flowered bowers, and the staff at the Hotel Girasole. Look, there's Beatrice coming out to meet us,' cried Caroline, and as Beatrice approached, Mel threw her wedding bouquet into the air for Beatrice to catch. Impulsively, Mel threw hers up in the air towards Izzy who jumped for it, then blushed pink as a bougainvillea blossom.

Beatrice had been cooking all the day before, and as they entered the lemon grove, there were tables laid out under starched white cloths. They were laden with a delicious antipasti of salami, tender asparagus, roasted peppers and tomatoes in fragrant olive oil, plump olives stuffed with anchovies and crisp, golden, deep-fried zucchini. Asti Spumante frothed overflowing into long-stemmed glasses and many toasts were drunk. Ravioli filled with crabmeat and lobster was served with spaghetti al burro sprinkled with the best flavoursome parmegiano. Vast dishes of curly baby squid with piquant dressing made from the lemons hanging from trees above them were followed by melt-in-the -mouth osso bucco in a rich sauce.

Finally, Beatrice wheeled out her finale dish. The torta mimosa alla Bavarese was greeted with a crescendo of applause. Banging on the table, Antonio's father, beaming from ear to ear, called for the raucous guests to raise their glasses in a toast. 'This wonderful cake cooked with affection will now be cut. In our very special Italian tradition the bride and groom, or should I say brides and grooms–.' The guests cheered and banged their cutlery on the table. ' — will feed each other with the first piece to signify a lifetime of sharing in one meal and the pledge to care for and love each other for all time.'

A moment of silence, a bird singing in the lemon tree above, the gentle rustle of Mel's and Caroline's silken skirts as they rose and each opened their mouths and took a piece of the sweet confection from their new husbands and fed them in return. The light sponge cake filled with Bavarian cream and sumptuously flavoured with vanilla melted on Mel's tongue and the deed was done, the pledge sealed. A tumultuous roar broke out among the guests. All was chatter and joking, drinking and, when Rafaele took out his mandolin to play Neapolitan love songs, spirited, lively, dancing. Even Antonio's father broke into a lusty baritone rendition of 'O Sole Mio.'

The guests did not filter away until the sun dropped low in the sapphire sky and the first stars appeared. Mel and Cesare embraced everyone, and thanked both Beatrice and Rafaele, and Antonio and Caroline profusely. Oscar was standing, waiting for Izzy to say goodbye to her friends. Mel, tired but happy, said with a tinge of sadness, 'Shall we make our way up to the hotel too? The only trouble is, Cesare, I don't want the day to end. I don't want to stop dancing, I don't want to take off my beautiful dress, I don't want to fall asleep, it's all been too wonderful.'

Cesare stroked her cheek. 'Then let us make it last a little longer, let's walk down to the shore, dip our aching feet in the cool waves and watch the sun rise over the sea.' As he raised a hand of farewell to Oscar and Izzy, Mel saw Oscar give her new husband a conspiratorial wink and wondered what that meant. Oscar was so generous, had he arranged a special breakfast treat for them for tomorrow morning back at the hotel? Or was his signal to Cesare something to do with their honeymoon? The honeymoon was all a big secret to her. Cesare had said he was going to take Mel somewhere lovely, but said he wanted to surprise her. Even now, suitcase packed, she had no idea where they were going. Perhaps Oscar had persuaded one of his international friends to lend them a flat somewhere exotic?

As they made their way down to the shore, kicked off their shoes and paddled in the water, Mel found herself looking back at the beach house. The Casa di Spiaggi, nestled at the bottom of Beatrice's lemon grove, looked over the wide moonbeam-scattered ocean. 'It is a very beautiful little house is it not?' murmured Cesare as his warm hand cradled her shoulder. Mel rested her head on his chest. She could hear his heart beat.

'It's the best house in the world, because it's the reason I came to Sorrento. Without coming here I wouldn't have met you. It looked such a sad little house when we came, with its shutters hanging off, and its rooftiles missing. Neglected and waiting for someone to come and make it whole again. When Oscar bought it, Caroline, Izzy and I had such fun repainting it and choosing curtains. That house reminds me a bit of myself.'

'How so, caramia?' Cesare kissed the top of her head.

'Well, I was in need of someone to come and repair me. I had a super job, in a loving family, but I was always like that little beach house. Waiting for someone special to come and make me whole.'

They'd reached the beach house now.

It stood with its windows reflecting the twinkling stars. Outside was a little bench. 'Let's sit for a moment.' Cesare helped her up onto the raised stone verandah and the two of them sat, looking to the left of them at the little house, to the right at the gently lapping wavelets. 'Can you smell these gorgeous lilies?' he said. White waxy regales wafted their delirious scent from terracotta pots. 'They are symbols of Venus, the goddess of love. And this pomegranate tree is like the ones planted by the Romans to signify marriage.' Basil flourished in a tiny flowerbed. He pinched it between his fingers. As the aroma teased her nose, it reminded Mel of the wife in Fazana who had joyfully held out her scented fingers to her husband as she was tending their plant pots and cooking him dinner.

'Oh Cesare, do you think Izzy might have planted this basil to send good wishes? And I'll bet Oscar put in these lovely new lavender plants. Lavender symbolises devotion.'

'It was not Oscar or Izzy.' Cesare

cupped her face in his strong, protective hands. 'It was me.'

'Have you taken to doing their gardening, among all your other talents?' She held his arms, feeling the strong muscles as he drew her closer.

'No, my darling caramia. I have never been much of a gardener, but I think I can learn, if it means creating a garden for my darling wife in our own little house.'

'What do you mean?' She held him tighter, as if today had all been too wonderful, too perfect and she might lose her grip on reality. This had all been such a dream.

'You must have been wondering, dearest Signora Mel Mazzotta, where we were to spend our honeymoon. Well, I hope you do not mind spending it right here, at the Casa di Spiaggia, at our own little house.'

'Ours?'

'Yes. I have bought it from Oscar, he gave me a very good price. On the one condition that he and Izzy can come and stay whenever they want, which I was most happy to promise. And I give it to you, my darling caramia. I love you with all my heart. Happy honeymoon. Here it is, our own little house by the sea.'

Mel's eyes welled with tears, tears of joy, which Cesare kissed away with a thousand kisses as he reached in his pocket and handed her the key. Her hand trembled as they opened the door and moonlight blessed them as they shared their first kiss, the first of many on the threshold of their beautiful house by the sea.

We do hope that you have enjoyed reading this large print book.

Did you know that all of our titles are available for purchase?

We publish a wide range of high quality large print books including:
Romances, Mysteries, Classics
General Fiction
Non Fiction and Westerns

Special interest titles available in large print are:
The Little Oxford Dictionary
Music Book, Song Book
Hymn Book, Service Book

Also available from us courtesy of Oxford University Press:
Young Readers' Dictionary
(large print edition)
Young Readers' Thesaurus
(large print edition)

For further information or a free brochure, please contact us at:
Ulverscroft Large Print Books Ltd.,
The Green, Bradgate Road, Anstey,
Leicester, LE7 7FU, England.
Tel: (00 44) **0116 236 4325**
Fax: (00 44) **0116 234 0205**

Other titles in the
Linford Romance Library:

HEART OF THE MOUNTAIN

Carol MacLean

Emotionally burned out from her job as a nurse, Beth leaves London for the Scottish Highlands and the peace of her aunt's cottage. Here she meets Alex, a man who is determined to live life to the full after the death of his fiancée in a climbing accident. Despite her wish for a quiet life, Beth is pulled into a friendship with Alex's sister, bubbly Sarah-Jayne, and finds herself increasingly drawn to Alex . . .

MIDSUMMER MAGIC

Julie Coffin

Fearing that her ex-husband plans to take their daughter away with him to New Zealand, Lauren escapes with little Amy to the remote Cornish cottage bequeathed to her by her Great-aunt Hilda. But Lauren had not even been aware of Hilda's existence until now, so why was the house left to her and not local schoolteacher Adam Poldean, who seemed to be Hilda's only friend? Lauren sets out to learn the answers — and finds herself becoming attracted to the handsome Adam as well.